STRAIGHT TO ETERNITY

I0552501

Onoma Series Prequel Novella

Alisa Hope Wagner

STRAIGHT TO ETERNITY

Onoma Series Prequel Novella

Straight to Eternity
Onoma Series Prequel Novella
Copyright © 2022 by Alisa Hope Wagner
All rights reserved.
Marked Writers Publishing
www.alisahopewagner.com

Scriptures taken from multiple translations of the Bible.

Author photo by Lori Stead of www.wetsilver.com
Cover images designed by Muhammad Ahsan Ayaz
Cover designed by Alisa Hope Wagner

ISBN-10: 1733433392
ISBN-13: 978-1-7334333-9-6

DEDICATION

Daniel, my high school sweetheart and soulmate.

Isaac, my first-born son and prophet.

Levi, my brown-eyed boy and shepherd.

Karis Ruth, my cherished girl and graceful companion.

Christina, my amazing twin.

ACKNOWLEDGEMENT

Writing this novella created in my heart feelings of both angst and ecstasy—angst every time I began a scene and ecstasy every time I finished it. The series I started seventeen years ago has now finally come to an end with this prequel novella. I had to go back to the almost four hundred thousand words of this series and pull theme threads, character arcs and plot closures into a novella of only thirty thousand words. And I have grown to love each character. They have both motivated me and wore me out.

I want to thank my husband who would listen to me whine about having to write this novella. "Just go write it!" he would say. Finally, I stopped stalling and began my wrestle with words, characters, scenes, themes and plots. I'm glad I listened to him. I also want to thank my two sons and daughter. They would listen to me yammer about my progress and offer their heartfelt congratulations. And, as always, the Holy Spirit worked with me, cheating on my behalf and giving me hints and clues for where the story should go and what the characters should do. Finally, I want to thank my editing team: Bernadine Zimmerman, Cynthia Faulkner, Daniel Wagner, Faith Newton, Jennifer Smith and Patricia Coughlin. I'm honored that you would take time to find those pesky typos and offer suggestions. Also, I want to thank Emerald Barnes for joining my editing team with your talent and expertise.

This is a work of speculative fiction. Names, characters, governments, languages, places, events and incidents are either the products of the author's imagination or used in a fictitious manner. Any resemblance to actual persons or actual events is purely coincidental.

INTRODUCTION

Fifteen years before the *Onoma Series* begins, the lives of two dissimilar characters collide, and they choose to trust a higher plan and work together to change the course of history. Christina Straight, a Life Therapist sentenced to serve six months in a prison for Efficientists women meets Jonah Goodman the Third, a young Colonial man who has just lost everything. A retired researcher, Matthew Coughlin, who helped develop the World Government's secret weapon has a hidden weapon of his own, and he uses it to formulate a two-part plan in a future hope to take down the World Government's tyranny. Now it is Christina and Jonah's task to ensure that the first part of this plan succeeds. However, they both must take risks and overcome past pains to move forward into a destiny that will alter the fate of millions for eternity.

"Make up your mind to live differently; praise your way to victory; give God the construction project; and understand that your history is not your destiny."
– Joyce Meyer

CHAPTER 1

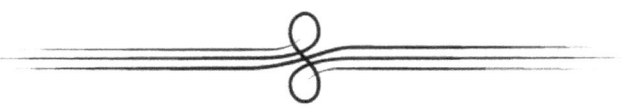

Christina Straight kept her expression even. She wouldn't allow the judicial committee to intimidate her, especially Neil Elder, who had scrutinized her work for years. He examined and dissected the history of her Life Production System (LPS) relentlessly, looking for any reason to convict her. Finally, the day came when his face popped onto her LPS screen unannounced, and he gave her the news that she would go to trial. He reveled in that moment just as he was reveling now.

Twelve windows for each member of the committee lined the right side of her LPS screen. She made sure to look at each image with a confident eye. They spoke in Long English, rather than the standard Twin Variety (T-variety) to avoid confusion. This shortened form of communication was useful when exchanging information, but they found that in court sessions, Long English was better because it left no room for doubt, misunderstanding and manipulation.

"Tell us yes or no, Ms. Straight. Was the Efficientist in question using Helpers to bump his rank?" Neil asked.

"As I have already stated numerous times, I am a Life Therapist and bound by a code of ethics. I will not discuss my client's personal or professional life with this committee." Christina noticed Neil's subtle smirk. She knew he was stalling the trial, trying to make her squirm. She wouldn't give him the satisfaction.

"If you do not answer my question on record, you will be sent to prison for a minimum of six months."

"Yes, I know," she said, willing her voice to stay strong. She didn't understand why God was allowing this to happen to her. She had been faithful to her calling, writing faith articles under the pseudonym of the Apostle. Her writings kindled the Efficientists Christian Sect, a movement of faith within the oppressive walls of *Life Efficiency*. Arthur Pallue, the creator of *Life Efficiency*, deemed faith worthless because it did not add to efficiency. When Neil Elder appeared on her screen that day, she thought he had finally discovered her true calling— spreading the Good News of Jesus Christ to Efficientists in all ten regions of the World Government. However, God ensured that her identity remained hidden. If He could protect her identity as the Apostle, why would He allow her to go to jail for withholding information? She didn't even like this particular client, and, yes, he was using Helpers to bump his rank, which she found deplorable. She could easily give him up. By law, she was required to answer this committee, yet the Holy Spirit told her in no uncertain terms not to give the information and that she would indeed be sent to prison.

One year. Suddenly, she felt it in her spirit. *One year.* God wanted her to postpone her sentence for a year.

"I am prepared to serve my prison sentence. I understand that I am breaking the law, and I will accept punishment for my crime. However, I counsel many Efficientists, and I need time to ensure that they continue in productivity per the requirements of *Life Efficiency*. I will need a year to complete therapy with them. I will not take any new clients until my sentence has been served."

Neil Elder quickly stifled his surprised expression. "You willingly go to prison? You do understand that you will be sent to the Colonies for this sentence?"

She nodded. She had never been to the Colonies. However, she had counseled a few Colonials who had become lower ranked Efficientists. The World News worked diligently to create a frightful and repulsive image of the Colonies, but she knew better. The World Government's control was centered on keeping Efficientists plugged into their LPSs every second of the day, striving to be productive and keep rank to gain fleeting value and purpose. But true value did not dwell in production.

"Does this committee agree?" Neil asked. "Christina Straight will be sentence to six months in prison for her crime of withholding information from the World Government, and the sentence will start a year from this date?"

Each committee's image glowed green on her LPS screen as he or she gave approval to the sentence. It didn't take long for eleven squares to be illuminated in favor of her sentence. They had more productive things to do than dwell on this simple case. Only Neil Elder waited, presumably agitated that the proceeding went along quickly, but he finally gave his approval and all twelve members voted for her prison sentence. She had a year. A year to wait for the inevitable, which also felt like a sentence.

"Fine, these proceedings are adjourned," Neil said. Suddenly, the eleven images of the judicial committee vanished from her screen. All that was left was Neil Elder.

"Why are you still here?" Christina asked. His face now occupied the space of the twelve.

Neil grinned. "I just wanted to let you know that we have enough evidence to convict your client. We don't need your testimony. He will be sentenced for using Helpers to raise rank."

"I couldn't care less," she stated matter-of-factly.

Neil's confused expression almost made her laugh, but she kept her smile under wraps. He was a prideful man, and she didn't want to give him more reason to hate her.

"You withhold information simply to vex me?"

"No. I withhold information because I am bound by a greater source."

"I know what you are, Christina Straight. You are a Christian. You tried to brainwash me when I sought you as my Life Therapist. I am glad I got out when I did. You could have had me drop rank like so many of your other clients. You think you are helping Efficientists, but you are a cancer to our way of life."

"I have never forced anyone to drop rank," she said calmly.

"Not outwardly, but subconsciously you seduce them with your words. You lead them down a path of self-discovering that unplugs them from the World Government and ends all true value they could have achieved. You almost had me convinced that life held more meaning than *Life Efficiency*. But production is the key to eternal life. The more we produce, the more destiny we claim."

She paused and stared at Neil. He had come to her several years ago when he and Arthur Pallue had a dispute that ended their relationship. "You should be glad that I keep my secrets. Or else I could let one slip about you," she said.

His cheeks and ears became crimson with anger.

"I know you hate that Arthur Pallue had a daughter late in life. You were his protégé, his favorite, until he decided to father a child. Now, Eve Pallue will quickly outrank you. She is almost an elite Efficientist and yet only in her teen years. There is a rumor that she's already working on a new Life Plan to surpass her father's *Life Efficiency*. Arthur Pallue created in his daughter the highest example of production, and you want her erased. Weren't those your exact words?"

"You dare blackmail me?" he demanded.

"No, I am not blackmailing. I'm merely pointing out that you are accusing me of the crime of withholding information when you yourself have benefited from it."

"I could arrange for you to never leave that prison," he whispered in anger.

"I'm sure you could and happily would," she said, feeling the weight of the moment. She needed to ensure she made it out of prison alive. God still had a purpose for her. The Holy Spirit had been slowly revealing the end purpose of her life. He told her that she would be part of an effort to rid the world of *Life Efficiency* once and for all.

She began to quickly type on her LPS keyboard. "I have our counseling notes from that day typed verbatim in a file on a Portable you will never find. And now—" she set a timer on the file—"if I am not back in my home in a year, six months and a day from now, that file will be sent in duplicate to the World Police. Therefore, you must ensure that I make it back on time and in one piece, or I will not be able to stop that file from being sent."

"There is no way you can do that! You don't have the clearance!" he yelled.

"You are willing to stake your life on that assumption? If I fear for Eve Pallue's welfare, isn't it my duty as a Life Therapist to warn the authorities and her father?"

Now Neil Elder's entire face beamed red. "Do not underestimate what I'm capable of, Christina Straight."

Christina allowed her face to mimic a concerned therapist's expression. A countenance she was accustomed to using in session with Neil Elder when she counseled him. "If you sent me there, then I would see first-hand your little labor secret."

"What are you insinuating?" he whispered. His face went from red to pale instantly.

"I know about your forced labor trial run in the Colonies."

"How dare you! Those are all rumors and lies!"

She shrugged pleasantly. "Maybe, but gossip is spreading."

"This conversation is over! You have one year! I want to go through eternity never seeing your face again!"

Neil's face vanished from Christina's LPS screen. "Well, you're in luck. I doubt I'll see you there anyway," she whispered to the dark screen, staring at her dim reflection. She could see faint, dark circles encasing the bottom lids of her eyes. She needed sleep. Finally, she exhaled and turned off the LPS with a verbal command. "Good riddance." Not having to deal with that man for the rest of her life was worth six months in prison.

Christina got up from her chair and began to pace her living room. She had much work to do. In a year, she would be imprisoned for six months and unable to write and publish her faith articles. If Neil Elder realized that the writings stopped while she served her prison sentence, he would connect the Apostle to her. She had exactly a year to write six months of extra material to be published with the Efficientists Christian Sect while she was away. Faith rose in her spirit, displacing all fear. God had a purpose in all things, including going to prison. Although she didn't fully understand all the details, she would trust that God knew what He was doing.

CHAPTER 2

Jonah interlocked the fingers of both his hands and tried to stretch out the ache. The wooden stool under him groaned as he tried to make his body comfortable after sitting for hours. Grabbing hold of the tiny wires on the motherboard was getting more difficult each day. He could easily manipulate them a few years ago, but his body had grown like the big pecan trees he once climbed when they didn't live in the factory. Now his fingers were thick and the skinny blue, red and yellow wires kept slipping through his grasp. His mamma said that he would be bigger than his papa soon, and she would often give him some of her evening food portions because the hunger pains hit him hard at night. He couldn't sleep when his stomach gnawed on the inside. He was tempted to steal a bit of ration when the guards went to sleep—that is until his friend was caught a few months ago. They never saw him again. They must have sent him back to the Colonies.

He eyed his little brother and sister on the other side of the assembly line table. His brother, Isaiah, was twelve and his sister, Maureen, was ten. They both had brown skin like himself, but his sister's coloring was a shade lighter matching their mamma's skin tone. Mamma tightly braided his sister's hair every week, using the stray rubber bands that tied the skinny bundles of wires together before they set them in place. He knew his brother and sister would be growing like the pecan trees too. At this stage, they could still easily pinch the wires and clamp them in place to the different cartridges. He figured soon he would be working next to his father, placing the large plastic lids over the encasements and fixing them in place with sturdy screws as fat as the brown roaches that scurried across the floor of the sleeping quarters each night.

Papa reminded him nightly that he would be leaving when he turned eighteen. He needed to plan where he would go after he left. They promised his papa, if they came to work for the factory, the kids could leave when they became of age. He was already seventeen years old and could leave in one more year. Jonah didn't know where he would go. Maybe back to the pecan trees and the river they once fished. His father and grandfather were proud fishermen. They always had fish to eat every night. But after the terrible freeze years back, most of the fish and trees died. Then the rains stopped, and his family didn't have enough food to eat and no fish or pecans to barter. That's when Papa brought them here. He wanted to make sure his kids could eat. Jonah rubbed his rumbling belly. He longed to eat pecans now.

He looked upstairs to where his mamma, Mary, sat on her own wooden stool at the women's assembly line. He couldn't see her, but he knew where she sat with the other ladies. She cut the plastic sections that would fit inside the big sleeping machines. He didn't know how the machines worked. He'd see the Runners as they carried them away in big boxes with dollies enroute to the city. Why would city folk sleep in plastic cases when they had soft beds? He shook his head. His family had never been to the city. It held too many scary tales. He even heard that nobody went outside. The government forced them—who they called the Efficientists—to work all day on big computer machines and then they slept at night in sleeping machines with hundreds of tiny, thin wires. He'd rather be in the factory than in the city. He heard that those Efficientists only slept about three hours a night. He was thankful for the six or seven hours he got.

A guard began making his way down Jonah's aisle with his rifle. He quickly went back to work. Whenever one of the guards caught him daydreaming, he would shove the butt of the rifle into his lower back. Not too hard to make him cry out but with enough force to cause a bruise. He didn't care so much about the bruises, but his mother did. He didn't want to add to her worry. He would hear her quietly crying to his papa some nights when they thought he was asleep. She'd opened Papa's old tackle box where she kept their family photos. There were not many of them because very few Colonials had cameras, but she had collected some through the years. They made her miss their old home. She didn't like the factory. She wanted to go back to the pecan trees and the river, but Papa insisted that they would die of starvation if they went back. Jonah disagreed. Spring had just begun, bringing with it new rains that would water the dried lands. And maybe the fish that were left after the freeze had begun to build back up again.

As the guard passed behind him, a girl's shriek ricocheted across the factory floor. Then a cacophony of screams rang out as wooden stools tumbled to the ground, and children began jumping onto the assembly table.

"Rattlers!" a guard yelled. "They're coming out of the vents!" Then rifle shots fired like a thunderstorm, scarring the grey walls and concrete floor with pockmarks.

Jonah stood and scanned the ground where the large, unused AC floor vents were located along the walls of the factory. He saw flashes of grey and black slithering out of several vents onto the concrete floor. The snakes were huge. Jonah felt his heart beating hard against his chest. The rattlesnakes must have taken the unused vents as a den for their brumation time. He stood, pushing his stool to the ground, adding to the chaos of the moment.

"Isaiah! Maureen!" Jonah cried. "Get on the table!" He watched as his sister and brother jumped onto the table, and wires and cartridges scattered onto the floor. More stools tumbled across the floor as the rest of the smaller kids began jumping onto the assembly tables.

"What is it?" the guard behind Jonah yelled. His rifle was against his left shoulder aiming toward the sea of kids.

"Don't shoot!" Jonah yelled. "It will only make the snakes madder, and you might shoot someone." Jonah had seen plenty of rattlesnakes near the pecan trees where they used to live. They would prey on the small animals that went after fallen pecans. They were hard to miss when they slithered by. As long as you didn't bother them, they didn't bother you.

"How'd they get in here?" he screamed.

Jonah felt the palpable fear of the guard. "There must be a den in the old AC vents. They're awake now for the season. They just want to get out."

Jonah scanned the ground. The snakes were heading toward them. They probably felt the warmth coming from the open factory doors behind them at the front of the factory. He looked up. He could see his mother holding onto the balcony railing looking down at them. Two guards stood at the top of the staircase, not letting any of the women come down. Jonah leaned onto the assembly table to jump on, but the flimsy table complained under his weight. "Just stay up there and don't move," he told his brother and sister. "The snakes are headed to the entrance. Don't give them a reason to bite you."

They nodded. His sister held tightly onto his brother's hand.

Jonah heard a loud thud and men's voices shouting. He looked to where his father was working in the smaller room to the left of the main area. They shut the huge, metal doors to his working section. His papa's deep, booming voice could not be muffled by doors. "Let me out! My kids are over there!" he shouted. A few shots of a rifle sounded off behind the doors and the yelling stopped. Suddenly, silence fell onto the factory floor and the rattle of snake tails vibrated from the ground. It sounded like hundreds of rattlers, but Jonah knew that the hard, factory walls echoed the sounds. He hoped only a dozen snakes were trying to make it out. Jonah grabbed his wooden stool from the ground. If one came up to him, he'd block an attack with it.

"Where are they? Where are they?" the guard behind him yelled nervously, still holding his rifle out.

Jonah wanted to tell the guard to be quiet, but the man was liable to shoot him. Then a click Jonah recognized sounded from the speakers overhead. It was the voice of the factory director, Neil Elder. "As you all now know, a den of snakes was discovered in the old central AC station in the basement. My guards were dissembling it for renovations when the snakes awoke. Please stay calm. Don't move. The factory doors are open. Let the snakes pass by. Guards, do not waste your ammo."

"Easy for him to say!" the guard behind him said. "He's safe up there in the watchtower!"

Jonah tried to inch away from the man, but he grabbed his shoulder. "Oh no! You are staying right here!"

His sister screamed. Jonah turned to see a huge rattlesnake rear up on his long body and slide his face onto the tabletop. His black, forked tongue scanned the air for scents. Jonah hoped that the snake's stomach was full of roaches and mice from the basement. It looked fat and fed, so hopefully, it wouldn't attempt an attack. The snake began to slither past the feet of his siblings coming toward him. He held up the stool and inched back slowly. The guard let go of Jonah and held the rifle back up to his shoulder.

"Don't shoot," Jonah whispered. "You're too close. That's for long-range."

"He's going to kill us," the guard squealed. "And they didn't give me a pistol! They don't have antivenom here. I'll die!"

Neil Elder's voice broadcasted again from the speakers. "Officer Taylor. Put your rifle down. That's an order."

Jonah looked at the small camera attached to the entryway to the main area of the factory. Director Elder must be watching them.

The snake raised its head and stared at Jonah over the stool. It seemed to grin sinisterly like it was about to steal from him. Jonah had nothing but his family. He didn't understand why, but at that moment, he knew the snake would strike. His heart began to pound faster, and he tried to control his breathing. He looked to his left and right. More snakes slid down the aisles on either side of him. There was nowhere he could go. The rattlesnake that singled him out caught onto one of the stool legs and began to wind its way up toward him. He wanted to throw the stool, but most of the snake's long body was still on the table next to his brother and sister.

"Stop it from coming!" the guard yelled.

"I can't!" Jonah yelled. "If I move, it'll strike!"

"Then I will!" the guard yelled.

Jonah felt a fierce push on his low back, and he tumbled forward with the stool. First, he felt the stool punch his gut as it crashed against the assembly table. Next, he felt a strike on his chest just below his neck. The snake's jaws clung to his body as he fell to the ground, and the sound of rifle shots pierced his ears. The last thing he saw as he lay on the ground with venom saturating his veins was his sister's body falling to the ground next to his. Blood poured out of her wounded chest in the same location of his snake bite. He watched her body shake as his chest began to burn and tighten. Finally, her quivering body stopped, and scarlet spewed out of her mouth with her last breath. "No!" he screamed and reached for her. The snake detached itself from his chest and struck again on his arm. He heard men shouting and more gunfire. Just before everything went black, the voice of his mamma called out his name. Then all went silent.

CHAPTER 3

Matt Coughlin shuffled into the spare bedroom of his small cabin. His body ached all over, and he felt weaker than the day before. He knew his condition would rapidly worsen. He stared at the young man sleeping on the bed. His skin was a little lighter than his dark umber tone, but the boy's hulking body was much bigger than his thin frame riddled with arthritis. It took all his strength to move the boy away from the piles of dead bodies during the night with one of the wheelbarrows left behind. He still had the wheelbarrow behind his cabin, and he hoped the security guards wouldn't miss it. Probably not. No one would care about a missing wheelbarrow when so much life was lost.

He had come to the field of bodies to look for a security guard—one he had been working with since he left the city and came to the cabin near the factory. To his horror, he saw his dead body lying aside two other security guards who had been either shot or bitten by the rattlers. Fear showed no favoritism—guards laid dead alongside the factory workers. Thankfully, he saw the young man's shallow breathing before he disappeared back to his cabin. All was not lost yet. At least he hoped. The young man had been bitten twice by a rattler and left for dead along with the other bodies strewn with bullet holes. A massacre. Over one hundred and fifty dead bodies rested on the free side of the fence of the forced labor camp. He noticed that the dead were organized by families. Probably for a final head count. He left a red, heart-shaped rock near the young man's dead family—a father, mother, brother and sister.

They were the first row of bodies several feet in front of the security fence. The boy would have questions, and Matt needed to give him the answers—regardless of how abysmal they were.

While the young man slept, Matt returned the following morning to what was quickly becoming a grave site, and he watched as security guards buried lifeless bodies in shallow graves. He was looking for the location of the young man's family. They buried his family where they lay the night before, not noticing that the young man's body was missing. Thankfully, the red stone remained unmoved. Matt felt anger rising like scorching air from his neck to his face even though the spring breeze was cool. He could still hear the bullet shots and the screams ripping through the forest the previous morning. His plan to destroy the World Government had been jeopardized. A plan he had meticulously designed for almost a year. It was flawless, but now the security guard he needed to accomplish the first part of the plan was dead. Matt walked over to the young man and examined the bite marks on his chest and arm. He had uncovered the wounds, so they could dry and heal. Thankfully, he thought to bring vials of antivenom along with his medicine when he left the city to live in the colonies almost nine months ago. After he had administered two vials to the boy, he only had one left. He wouldn't use it for himself even if he did finally get bitten. He had other means of dying quickly, but now he needed this boy to live. Matt was already developing a new plan, and it would have to include this young man. It was time for him to pass the baton.

He had helped create the Kill Switch along with Neil Elder and a few other Efficientists It was in the watchtower of the forced labor camp where Neil and his guards kept constant surveillance. He reached into his pocket and felt for the silver cartridge that rested between the fabric of his worn pants. The cartridge had an undetectable virus implanted in it. He spent his entire life working for Arthur Pallue, the founder of *Life Efficiency*, trusting his decisions for a better, safer New America—one region in an all-powerful World Government. But it was all a lie. Arthur Pallue was a hypocrite, and his daughter was following unwaveringly in his footsteps. She would ultimately lead people into a life of slavery to the World Government by living a life of endless production. He knew she was working on a new Life Plan to surpass her father's *Life Efficiency*. She was still young yet. Probably the same age as the young man he saved. It may take her ten or more years to finish her work. However, time was irrelevant. The second half of his plan to take down the World Government could wait in hibernation until all the pieces fell into place.

He stared at the young man's face. Like all the prisoners at the forced labor camp, his parents had gone willingly. That was another sort of enslavement but for the Colonials—giving up personal freedom to live with a sense of safety. The World Government had developed two methods of control—production for the Efficientists and security for the Colonials. Old America's collapse caused by the public-school riots had birthed a spirit of fear from the devastation. Consequently, New America rebuilt itself into a web-world of servitude to a world system greedy to dominate. Instead of freedom, New America was simply one of ten regions that shared money points, a World Police and a World News centered on manipulation and control. However, his knowledge of the Kill Switch and the secret weapon he discovered would take the World Government down by erasing everything from banking systems to personal sites to the smallest files of information. Nothing would be left and the false authority the World Government claimed would disappear in an instant.

A deep sting pierced Jonah's chest. When he tried to reach for it, he felt another sting in his arm. His entire body was tired and worn like he had run nonstop for days in the heat with no water. He opened his eyes, but the light in the room caused him to squeeze them shut. He wanted to speak, but his dry throat couldn't produce a sound. Suddenly, a glass rim came to his mouth and cool water touched his lips. He began to drink the water deeply. The liquid felt cool dripping down his chin and onto his chest.

"Mamma," he whispered without opening his eyes. "Is everyone okay? Did they take care of Maureen?"

He heard a man's voice he did not recognize. "What is your name, son?" the man asked.

Jonah knew when he was asked a question, he'd better answer back. "Jonah Goodman the Third," he replied. "How is my sister, Maureen. And Isaiah? Are they okay?"

Jonah's stomach tightened. The man's voice hesitated and Jonah sensed there was something wrong. He wasn't in his sleeping quarters. The bed under him was soft, not like the hard floor of the factory basement. And the sweet scent of trees and grass replaced the smell of burning plastic and wires.

"There was an incident at the factory," the man said softly. "But before I explain it all, let me tell you about myself. Can you open your eyes? I closed the curtains. The room is no longer so bright."

Jonah blinked a few times and focused on where the voice was coming from. He saw an old man standing above him. He was much too old to be working the factory. He didn't sound like a factory worker either, but he also didn't sound like a guard.

"Who are you? Where am I?"

The old man stood next to a wooden chair by the bed. His skin was dark like his papa's, but he was small and frail. The old man winced as he sat down like he was in pain.

"Did you get bit by one of them rattlers too?" Jonah asked.

The man laughed and shook his head. "No, I'm just an old man with aching bones. My name is Mathew Coughlin, but you can call me Matt. I worked at the factory a few years ago before the Colonials were brought in."

"Did you design those sleeping machines, Mr. Matt?" Jonah asked. "Are you an Efficientists? Did you come from the city?"

"Yes, I am an Efficientist," Matt said. "And I did come from the city, but I didn't design Sleepers. I helped design something quite different."

"I've never met an Efficientist besides Neil Elder, the director of our factory. Sometimes they come into the factory, but they always go straight to the watchtower. None of them have ever stopped to talk to us."

"I'm a retired Efficientists," Matt said and hesitated. "I know Neil Elder. I used to work with him. He's not a very good man."

Jonah shrugged. "He doesn't seem to be good or bad—just doing his job, I guess."

"You say that because you don't know what he has done and is still doing. Remember the young man that was caught stealing rations several months ago?"

Jonah nodded. "Yes. No one knows where he is."

"That's because he's dead. Neil Elder had him executed for stealing."

Jonah tried to get up but winced. "He can't do that!"

"He can, and he does. I need to tell you something."

Jonah's stomach tightened even more. "Where is my sister? She was hurt." An image of blood spraying out of his sister's mouth came to his mind. His stomach wrenched and he dry heaved.

"You are going to have to calm your breathing," Matt said. "Listen to my voice. Breath in deeply through your nose and hold your breath four counts. Good, now let out your breath in four counts. Do it a few more times until you feel your heart begin to slow down."

Jonah did what he was told, but tears began to flow from his eyes. "I don't want to listen to you if you've got something bad to tell me. Is it bad or good 'cause I don't want to hear a bad ending to your story!"

"It's very bad, but it doesn't have to end that way. It can have a good ending if you listen to my plan. You've been spared because you have a purpose that only you can accomplish. When you are done with your part of the plan, you will have that good ending you want."

"Is my sister dead?" Jonah asked. He closed his eyes again. He wanted to go back to sleep where the pain couldn't touch him.

"Yes, she is dead."

Jonah sat up ignoring the pain that shot through his body. He stared into the old man's dark brown eyes. "What about my brother? Is he okay?"

The old man leaned back and sighed, staring down at his wrinkled hands. Then he returned Jonah's gaze. "If I tell you, promise me you will give me a minute before you react. Just listen to what I have to say before you make any move. Promise?"

Jonah didn't want to promise. He wanted to get up and go back to his family at the factory, but he couldn't go back if what the man had to say was bad. His stomach jerked again, and this time bitter water spewed out of his mouth and onto the blanket laying over his legs.

"Jonah," the old man said, grabbing his arm with withered fingers, "you must promise me you will not leave this bed after I tell you everything. If you do, you will never have that good ending I told you about!"

Jonah wiped the bitter water from his chin with his uninjured arm. "Tell me the good first! I need to hear the plan you have that leads to good!"

Matt patted the young man's arm. "Yes, you are right. I will tell you the good first." The old man sat wearily back into the chair. "I have a plan to destroy the World Government, so they never make forced labor camps again. That is where you and your family have lived these past years, not just a factory. You and other Colonials lived in a forced labor camp. It was not a good place to live regardless of what they told you. They were exploiting all of you—even young children—to work for free. The World Government is running low on oil because Old America tried to stop the production of it, so now they are planning on making Colonials like you their replacement for energy."

Jonah shook his head. "I don't know what that word means, *exploiting*."

"It means that they are using you. It means that at any time they can do what they want with you—even bad things. They feed you and give you a place to sleep, so now they think they own you. You are no longer free. You are forced to do labor, to work for them."

Jonah looked away from the old man. No matter what his father had said about how the factory took care of them, he had felt a great loss. He now realized that the loss was his freedom.

The old man continued. "Neil Elder is a very bad man. He is the one who started up the forced labor camps, and he has plans to create more of them. If he gets too much power, he will do many more bad things to Colonials."

The image of the factory director came into Jonah's mind. He felt a rush of anger for him that he had never experienced before. "I hate Neil Elder!"

The old man nodded. "And that you should. He needs to be stopped, along with the entire World Government. That is why I need you. I had a perfect plan to take it all down, but that plan has now been compromised. However, I am creating a new plan that I want to give you, so you can have that good ending. It is not by accident that you are here today. I need you to help me, and I in return will help you."

A numbness crept over Jonah's mind, suffocating the tension in his body. The pain in his arm and chest vanished, as he tucked all his emotions into a point of hatred toward Neil Elder. Jonah looked back at the man's aged face. "Why was your plan destroyed? What did Neil Elder do after the rattlers invaded the factory floor?"

The old man sighed again. "After the shootings stopped, he had the rest of the workers executed to ensure the news about the incident would not get out. One bodyguard that died in the initial crossfire was a man who I was working with. He was supposed to implement the first half of my plan that evening when Neil Elder slept. This massacre was very unexpected and threw my entire plan onto a different trajectory. You only survived because they left you for dead. I found you and brought you back here to my cabin and administered antivenom to you. You've been asleep for three days."

"My family is gone. That's a very bad ending." Jonah's hands balled into fists. "Does your good ending include the death of Neil Elder?"

"Killing him won't stop the World Government from doing this again. Another power-hungry Efficientist will take his place. Killing a single man is small. Killing the entire World Government is the only plan that will give you a truly good ending. And that is the plan I want you to inherit—or, at least, part of it."

"Can your plan include killing Neil Elder and destroying the World Government at the same time?" Jonah asked. "I don't care about this government. I only care about him."

Matt slowly stood up. "Look, there is more at stake than you realize. There is something bigger than you're able to see right now. You are young, but I will try to help you to understand all the good my plan will achieve. It will free everyone—Efficientists and Colonials. And I will make you a promise. You won't have to achieve this plan alone. I think I have found someone to help you from inside the factory. I'll bring her here and together you can accomplish my plan. I know every inch of that factory," Matt said, walking to a desk against the wall. He took out a large, folded paper from the drawer. Jonah noticed a machine on the desk that he didn't recognize.

Matt walked back to the bed. "You see this? This is a map of the outside and inside of the factory. I will ensure that my plan is flawless. Plus, I have a secret weapon that the World Government knows nothing about. It gives me both access and power to the systems of the World Government."

Jonah listened as Mr. Matt's words continued. He nodded and whispered affirmative words, but he had already decided in his heart that if there was any chance to kill Neil Elder, he would take it. That was the only good ending that would help ease the pain of losing his entire family. When the talking stopped, Jonah looked up.

"I see I have given you too much information for now," Matt said. "Why don't you get some sleep? I have some work I need to do." Matt walked back to the desk and sat on the chair. He returned the map to the drawer and turned on the unknown machine.

Jonah watched the old man type for several minutes until the rhythm of the clicks lulled him back to sleep.

CHAPTER 4

Jonah stared at the graveyard and then turned to look at Matt who stood a few paces away from him. He had to practically carry the old man from the cabin to the gravesite. Jonah noticed that as he got stronger each day, the old man was getting weaker. He brought his gaze back to the graveyard, desperately trying to wipe away the tears that flooded his eyes. He once looked longingly at this field on the other side of the fence as a place he would love to explore, but now it was filled with the bodies of his family and friends. The heart-shaped, red stone marked where his family was buried: Jonah Goodman the Second, Mary Goodman, Isaiah Goodman and Maureen Goodman. The numbness he felt broke a little, allowing a heave of pain to tighten his chest.

"Thank you for marking their graves," he mumbled.

"It was the least I could do," Matt whispered. "You have lost a lot. I can only hope that what I have to offer you will renew your hope in life and give you purpose."

Jonah had a singular purpose in mind, but there was no use arguing about it with the old man. He wanted Neil Elder dead. He looked toward the factory. The sun was high overhead. "Are you sure the guards won't see us out here? It's broad daylight."

Matt shook his head. "They are getting the factory ready for a few new changes."

"What changes?" Jonah asked.

Matt gave a mischievous grin that Jonah had grown accustomed to over the past few days. It meant he had a secret.

"I used my special weapon to manipulate the system. First of all, they are moving the Sleeper machinery to a factory closer to the city. This will save the Runners time and fuel taking the Sleepers back and forth such a distance. This factory is extremely remote, which was why we chose to build the Kill Switch here."

"Why would you care if the Runners save time? They work for the World Government," Jonah said.

"The changes I make must be sound or the World Government will become suspicious of the orders I'm giving. I don't want people asking questions. I bounce the orders through different official channels, so they don't have a firm understanding of who is sending them. But they are official—or at least, appear so. Orders must have adequate reasons for change, so they won't be questioned."

"What are the other changes?"

"Second of all, the factory will begin cultivating cotton. This place is surrounded by hundreds of acres of old farmland. They'll grow, harvest and process it. They'll be here just in time to plant the first harvest in early spring."

"Are they going to take more Colonials as their workforce?" Jonah asked. Seeing this factory being used as another forced labor camp caused the anger he carried deep down to flare up. He balled his fist as an image of Neil Elder's body lying on the factory floor with blood spewing from his mouth filled his mind. The image gave him a strange sense of peace.

Matt must have noticed his reaction because he placed his wrinkled hand on his shoulder. "No, he has shelved the idea of using forced labor for now. His idea must lay low for a while until any rumors of what happened here passover. The World Government still has some oil reserves. I figure they'll get desperate in ten to twenty years for human labor once more."

"So then who is going to work the fields?"

"The factory will become a women's prison for Efficientists and Colonials who work for the World Government. They'll serve their time working the cotton as penance for whatever they did to anger the World Government. Then they will go home. The work is tedious but not difficult."

"I'm surprised. I didn't figure Efficientists went to jail," Jonah said.

"Efficientists and Colonials are all equal in the eyes of the World Government. We simply have different roles to play. And honestly, the factory needs to have a front to prevent knowledge of the Kill Switch from leaking out. Very few people know it is there, so the factory must stay active to give Neil Elder and his team a reason to continue overseeing it."

"What exactly is a Kill Switch?" Jonah finally asked. He had heard Mr. Matt repeat that word several times. "You helped build it?"

Matt nodded. "It is a failsafe in case the World Government's systems become compromised. It continuously saves copies of all the systems, sites and files. Once the Kill Switch is pulled, it will reboot everything to where they were last saved. It's never been tested though."

"Why did they have you make it?"

Matt placed a frail hand in his pocket and brought out a shiny, silver cartridge. "Because Arthur Pallue wants to protect the society he has created. But this little cartridge," he said, holding it up so Jonah could see, "has a virus that will erase it all. It is the first step of my plan. I was supposed to meet my security guard the night of the massacre and give it to him. Our plan was finally ready to be implemented. He was going to pull the Kill Switch and insert the cartridge into the terminal. Then the reboot would have my virus undetected and dormant until the right time."

"They would have known he pulled the Kill Switch. There are cameras everywhere."

"It wouldn't matter. He would have been gone before they figured out what was going on."

"What was he going to do? Walk out the front gate? They would have shot him before he even left the factory! Is that what you are planning for me to do? Risk my life for your plan?"

"Of course not," Matt said, offended. "I told you I was working on another plan for you. Plus, he wouldn't have walked out the front door. We devised a way for him to get out undetected. It took us nine months, but we were finally ready."

"But even if he did get out, he could never go back to work. He's a security guard who works for the World Government. How would he survive in the Colonies with no money points or anything to barter? He couldn't go back home to his family. He'd have to completely disappear."

"Exactly," Matt said.

"And let me guess. You had that all planned out too?"

Matt gave another one of his wrinkled grins. "That is a discussion for another time. Let me give you two more pieces to my new plan," he said, placing the cartridge back into his pocket. "When the women's prison opens, there will be an Efficientist coming who will help you. I've already contacted her. I was looking for someone intelligent and sympathetic to our cause."

"You mean, your cause," Jonah interjected.

"It's a cause for all humanity, Jonah. And I hope it will soon become your plan as well."

"I don't see how that is possible."

"Trust me. Now back to her. She is a miracle. I couldn't have found someone more perfect. And the fact that she has been sentenced to jail is even more of a miracle because her record is spotless—though, I know something about her that not a single soul on this earth knows."

"Let me guess. Your secret weapon?"

"Precisely," Matt said.

Jonah tried to conceal his confusion. Even if he wanted to help with Mr. Matt's plan, he could barely understand it all. Everything Mr. Matt said seemed to create more questions in his mind. "And she's supposed to help me pull the Kill Switch?"

"Neither of you will have to pull it."

Jonah scratched the back of his neck and did not attempt to hide his confused expression from showing itself. "I don't understand you, Mr. Matt. It's like you speak in riddles."

"All she needs is the old-style computer that I have on my desk."

"Is it that machine you have been working on? An old computer, like from Old America days?"

"Precisely. It is my secret weapon. It has the anchor virus for the spreader virus I placed on the cartridge. They are like magnet and metal bringing everything together."

"But how am I supposed to give it to her? They're not going to let me just walk in. They think I'm dead. And since I'm not, they'll definitely shoot me."

Matt reached his hand into his other pocket. "Remember that map I showed you?"

"Yes," Jonah said, eying the large, folded paper.

Matt opened it. "You see this?"

"It looks like some kind of pipe underground that you added to the map," Jonah said, tilting his head to get a better view. "It leads under the factory walls."

"This is the tunnel that my security guard had been working on for the last nine months. It starts at a large unused air conditioning duct on the bottom floor near the front door and goes several feet just outside the factory wall. He dug it as often as he could when he worked the night shift. It's only about eight feet long. It would have taken him much less time to dig, but he had to be extremely careful."

Jonah thought. "I see those air condition ducts everywhere. That's where the rattlers came slithering out."

"And the AC leads all around the inside of the factory walls. In fact, there is one in the watchtower that leads down to the factory level."

"I understand now. He was going to pull the Kill Switch, add your cartridge and then sneak back into the air conditioning duct. Then make his way down to the factory floor and escape through the tunnel."

"Yes, and by the time he made it through the gate, he would be long gone."

"Is that what you are going to have that Efficientist woman do? Add the cartridge once it is pulled and make her way out?"

"No, that is what you are going to do," Matt said with finality.

"But the tunnel is way over there. And I'm way over here," Jonah said, getting frustrated.

"Yes, it is. You will have to dig your own tunnel from here and link it to the one on the other side of the factory."

Jonah looked past the security fence to the factory wall. It was at least 500 or 600 feet away or more. "But that would take years!" Jonah protested.

"It can only take one year."

"Why a year?"

Matt refolded his map and slipped it back into his pocket. "Because that is when the women's prison opens and your new friend arrives. Until then, the security here will be very sparse. I'm sure Neil Elder will send most of the security guards to the new Sleeper plant closer to the city with strict orders to say nothing about what happened here. He'll keep only his core team with him."

Digging a tunnel for the next year sounded worse than forced labor. "I don't know. There is so much I don't understand. How am I going to survive here an entire year?"

"Don't worry about a thing. I will provide for you," Matt assured him.

Jonah looked around at the ground. "Where would I start digging?"

"Right there," Matt pointed. "Right where I placed the red stone. It will be a straight shot to the tunnel by the factory wall."

"You want me to dig a tunnel next to my family's graves?"

"Don't you think that it's fitting? You dig your own grave next to your family's, but instead of leading to death, yours will lead to the downfall of the World Government, bringing life to the world."

Jonah held up his hands and backed up a few steps, but he suddenly stopped. If he could get into the factory undetected, he could easily find Neil Elder and take him out. He didn't care about this Efficientist woman or Mr. Matt's plan, but he now had true motivation to dig the tunnel.

"Look, I know this is difficult, and the waiting will be long, but the Efficientist coming, Christina Straight is a Life Therapist."

"What does that mean?" Jonah asked.

"It means that she can help you work through the trauma of losing your family. She's a doctor for the mind and heart. She will help you heal from your pain."

"Okay, I'll do it," Jonah said. But it wouldn't be Christina Straight that healed him. It would be the death of Neil Elder.

Matt gave a smile of relief. "Good. My first plan is secure. I will give you more of the details in the days to come. But you better start digging right away. I have a shovel at the cabin, and we can use the wheelbarrow in the back to bring the dug-up soil back into the forest. You will need to find a large enough stone to cover the hole you create, so people won't become suspicious. In fact, you should make it look like a gravestone."

"Mr. Matt, can I make a gravestone for all my family?"

Matt rubbed his chin. "I don't know. The security guards may become suspicious."

"But you said yourself that most of those security guards are leaving. The last thing they'll want to do is visit this place, reminding them of all the wrong they committed. Let me do it now, so when the new security gets here, they'll think they were already here."

Matt took a few more seconds to think. "Actually, you may be right. It would seem odder to have a single gravestone, and they might check it out and discover our tunnel. Okay, do it quickly. Take the wheelbarrow and find your stones in the forest. I have a few sharp knives you can use to carve their names. But first, help me back to the cabin. I have more work I need to do."

CHAPTER 5

Jonah returned to the cabin late in the evening. He set the shovel against the wall and left the wheelbarrow near the backdoor. His hands were blistered, and he had thick mud all over his body. But somehow the burden of the pain he carried lifted slightly. He didn't know where precisely the security guards buried each of his family members, but he lovingly placed a gravestone with his family's names on each one down the line about four feet apart from each other in front of the red, heart-shaped stone that Mr. Matt had left. In a graveyard of over a hundred and fifty bodies, the Goodman name would at least be known. He started digging while talking to the graves of his father, mother, brother and sister who were right there with him. His *freedom grave* as Mr. Matt called it was about three feet in front of his family's. He was impressed with how fast he could dig. It was like working the factory with his family nearby. Instead of sitting and pinching tiny wires, however, he stood and slung dirt. He felt free, and he tried not to look too far ahead. If he simply dug the dirt in front of him, the tasks didn't seem too overwhelming.

"You are really late," Matt said as Jonah opened the cabin's back door. "Stay out there and wash off in that bucket of water that I had you bring from the creek. Here's a washcloth."

Jonah grabbed the rag and took off his boots and clothes. Then he dunked the rag into the bucket of water and scrubbed at his mud-caked body. At the end of his washing, he placed one foot at a time into the water and rinsed them with his hands.

"Now here's my robe." Matt handed him the robe from the other side of the door. "I forgot you don't have a change of clothes. Just use that for now."

"Thank you, Mr. Matt," Jonah said, wrapping the robe around his large frame. The fabric barely closed shut. Before entering the living room, Jonah reached into the wheelbarrow and pulled out a shiny box.

"What took you so long? And what is that box you have?" Matt asked, sitting on the small couch. There were two large oil lanterns on the small table in the middle of the room, giving off just enough light.

Jonah could tell Matt was in a lot of pain. He smelled the whiskey on his breath when he handed him the robe. Not too much, though. The alcohol would ease the pain of his body, but Mr. Matt never wanted to dull his wits.

"I found something. It's like one of those miracles you talked about when you found that Efficientist lady with the old-style computer machine of yours."

"I'll be," Matt said, slapping one of his knees. "Jonah Goodman, you are smiling. I have never seen you smile. It looks good on you."

Jonah instantly relaxed his mouth. He didn't want Mr. Matt to know he had been talking to his family today. Maybe it was weird, but it felt good to chat about everything that had happened since he moved into the cabin. And there were no security guards to yell at him to shut up or to shove the butt of their rifle into his back. He held the box and walked to the armchair adjacent to the small couch and sat, placing the box on his lap.

"This is my papa's tackle box," Jonah began, trying to minimize the excitement in his voice. "Mr. Matt, where you put that red stone is where I started digging. It didn't take long for my shovel to hit something. When I finally got it out, I discovered that security guards must have buried all the workers' belonging, including this. Your rock was placed right over my papa's tackle box."

Matt looked intrigued and leaned forward. "What's in it?"

"We didn't have much, but my mom saved photos that were taken of us throughout the years. When I went to the Colonial school for a bit, a woman came by and took our pictures. Then, we went to this church for a while before it burned down. They took a photo of me and my brother and sister. Later, my papa's friend bartered for a camera and film equipment and took a photo of all of us at our river. You see?" Jonah said, handing the photo to Mr. Matt. "This is where we lived before we moved here. That's the river my grandpa, my papa and I would fish in. And those trees would drop pecans in the fall that my little brother and sister would pick up. They'd even crawl up the trees to get them."

"It is such a lovely place. I don't want to question your father's motives, but why did your family move to the factory?" Matt asked, handing the photo back to Jonah.

Jonah gently took the photo and placed it in the tackle box and closed the lid, locking it in place. He leaned back allowing his mind to fill with memories. "I never knew we were poor until I went to that Colonial school for those few weeks. The kids made fun of me. I hated it, so my mom brought me home and taught me and my brother and sister to read using sticks in the dirt. We even did math that way. My family didn't live in a nice cabin like this one. We lived in these make-shift homes. They were easy to make and just as easy to tear down. They kept the wind and bugs out at night when we slept, but we were outside most of the day. We were happy. We fished the waters, ate what we caught and bartered with the extra fish. The pecans too. People always wanted those. Anytime, I wanted a snack, I'd crack a few. I never felt hungry. But we always had to be careful about the gangs. There were several of them and they were always on the move. They would come into your land with these loud cars and trucks without warning and take everything you owned. Since we didn't have much, we could get up and leave during the night right when we heard their engines. Then we would return days later when they had gone, and we would rebuild our little huts."

"Are the gangs why you came to the factory? Did they threaten you?" Matt asked.

"They weren't that bad—not until the freeze came. When the freeze came, almost all the fish in the river died. It never got too cold where we lived. We had blankets for those cooler days, but this freeze was different. The people nearby let us stay in the school. It was still cold, but at least we could lay together with our blankets. When the freeze left a week later, we returned to our part of the river, and the fish were belly up. And they smelled so bad. But the pecan trees didn't die. They were sturdy." Jonah stopped talking and lost himself in memory.

"So you could still harvest the pecans?" Matt prodded. "And you stayed longer?"

"Yes, for two more years," Jonah said, coming out of his reverie. "Everything before the freeze was wonderful. I have so many great memories before that time, but the summer after the freeze, the rains dried up. It was the hottest two summers I can remember. Our river became a small creek. No more fish. My mom couldn't plant her garden. And the pecan trees suffered. We had to be creative. We may still be there, but the gangs were getting hungry. With all the plants dying, most of the animals began to die, too. Then people became desperate and scary and would do monstrous things. That's when my papa heard a rumor about a factory that would take you in for work. We had been there for over two years before–" Jonah stopped.

"Before the incident," Matt finished. "I see why your family went to the World Government for help. I wish

I could say that they had your family's best interests at heart, but they don't. They are corrupt, and they exploited you. They should have taken you in, and when you wanted to leave when things became safer in the Colonies, they should have let your family go back home. You trusted them, and they abused that trust. That is why they must be stopped."

Jonah said nothing. He held the tackle box close to his chest.

Matt waited for a bit before getting up. "Since you trusted me with your family photos, I'm going to trust you with something of mine."

Jonah looked up. "More of your plan?"

"Yes and no." Matt laughed. "You do tire of me talking about the plan. You've been a great sounding board for me. I know I confuse you a bit, but you've really helped me sort out some details."

Matt walked over to his room and disappeared. When he came back through the doors, he was holding something that Jonah recognized.

"That is a Portable. I saw Neil Elder carry his around all the time. I've never seen him without it. I've been meaning to ask you. How are you able to operate that machine and that Portable without electricity?"

"I have a small generator in the back," Matt said.

"What's that?" Jonah asked.

Matt laughed again. "Now I know why I confuse you so often. You really did grow up simply, but not in a bad way. I think you had a beautiful upbringing. Much better than mine, that is for certain. The generator is the machine in the back making that humming noise. It powers everything I have that needs electricity, and it charges my batteries."

"Oh," Jonah said. He looked at the aged man's face. "What was *your* childhood like?"

Matt slowly sat back down on his couch holding his Portable. "I grew up in an infamous LLC before they abolished them."

"What is an LLC?"

"Learning Life Center. All learning. No affection. No love. No touch. Simply a transfer of information from teachers to students in hopes that someday we would be proficient producers. Luckily, I had a few teachers who showed me tenderness. Otherwise, I would have wound up like so many of the other students who grew up in that system."

"What happened to them?" Jonah asked.

"They are either dead or insane, and since the World Government doesn't like to deal with people who do not produce, I can make a fair assumption that they are all dead along with anyone else who is deemed a burden on society."

"My papa was right," Jonah whispered. "The city is a scary place."

Matt shook his head. "Jonah, it is not the cities or the Colonies that are scary. In Old America, we had both urban and rural places that were both pleasant. It is a corrupt, all-powerful One World Government."

Jonah winced. He didn't want Mr. Matt to continue his talk about the government.

"I know. I know. You don't want to hear about it. But that is not why I brought my Portable to you. Here," Matt said, patting the seat next to him on the small couch. "Sit next to me. I have something for you."

While Jonah set his tacklebox on the ground and got up, he noticed Mr. Matt had already turned on his Portable with his thumb. Something, Neil Elder did often. Jonah sat down on the couch and listened as Mr. Matt gave weird, short commands that he didn't understand while pushing buttons on the keyboard.

"What is it that you are saying?" Jonah asked.

"It's Twin-variety or T-variety as we call it. It's a condensed form of Long English. You must speak T-variety to command the Portable."

"And people speak this language in the city?"

"They trained us at the LLC to speak it. Supposedly, Author Pallue's daughter, Eve, is the first native speaker of T-variety. It relies on the fact that the listener and speaker share information."

"And it works?" Jonah asked, skeptically.

"It does a good job at transferring information, but if you wanted to tell a joke or a sad story, it will not convey emotions beyond the descriptions of them. Meaning you can tell the joke or story, but no emotional response will occur by the listener—just understanding."

"People in the city don't laugh or cry?"

"The lower Efficientists do. They give up on higher ranks for quality of life. But the upper Efficientists, like me, we gave up all quality of life for quantity of production. That, my boy, is *Life Efficiency*. I never married. I never had kids. I never laughed or cried. I simply worked—except if I was at a Public Relations Event to build my poll ratings. The public must approve of you, or you can lose rank. This is what I mean when I say my life was stolen from me. I have nothing to show for it but a high rank, money points and a Kill Switch that I helped build and will use to destroy it all."

Jonah nodded. Some of what Mr. Matt was saying started to make sense to him. Mr. Matt may have never been trapped in a factory working on skinny wires, but he was trapped in other ways.

Matt placed the Portable in front of Jonah. "Place your thumb on the print identifier."

Intrigued, Jonah placed his right thumb on the small glass disk.

"Good. Now you are my bodyguard, and your life is irrevocably connected to mine."

"What does that mean?" Jonah asked. "Bodyguard?"

"They are like personal assistants and protectors of upper Efficientists. I am able to limit or give you limitless access to my Portable and everything therein. I just gave you unlimited access."

"That means you gave me all access?" Jonah asked. "Why would you do that?"

"I'm dying, Jonah. I won't make it the full year here. I don't think I'll make it a few months. You will be here alone to complete the first part of the plan. The second part of the plan is set. Christina Straight has all the information, and she will help you once she gets here. There are a few things she must sort out, but she is one intelligent, innovative woman. I've had several correspondences with her, and truly, she is like a gift sent from God."

"Do you believe in God?" Jonah asked. He had never heard Matt mention His name.

"I used to not, but I'm reading a lot of her faith writings. They are causing me to ask questions that I never dared to ask before. This won't make sense to you, but she has an alter ego."

"What is that?"

"It means she goes by another name and does another job. To the World Government, she is Christina Straight, Life Therapist who is helping Efficientists reach peak performance. However, underground in the web-world, she goes by the Apostle. She has been publishing faith writings for years and has never been caught. I don't know how she has kept it under wraps for so long, but they'll eventually discover her, which is why I want her to have my old-style computer. Once she has that secret weapon, they'll never find her."

"And it will help her to finish the second part of your plan?" Jonah asked.

"You are catching on, my son," Matt said.

Jonah felt heat rise from his cheeks. His father called him that. It felt good to hear it again.

"But how can I use your Portable once you are gone?"

"The World Government only notices deaths when production stops. After a year of non-production, they will confiscate everything, especially the money points. For this reason, parents will usually give access to their Portables or LPSs—that's the Life Production Systems we use when at home—to their kids before they die. If my Portable continues to be used, the system assumes the user is still living. I gave you all authority. Continue using it. All my money points are yours. I will teach you how to use the basic settings, so you can buy supplies at the nearby trading center. I can already see you need to purchase gloves for digging. Your hands are torn up."

Jonah looked down at his blistered hands. "They are starting to hurt more."

"It's because the endorphins from your hard work are wearing off. The exercise of digging will be good for you. It will keep your energy up. When Christina Straight gets here, she can teach you more."

"But how will I find her?" Jonah asked, now feeling for the first time the weight of what he was doing. He wasn't expecting Mr. Matt to give him all his money points.

"She knows about the tunnel. She'll make sure to meet you on nights when no one is looking. The security of a women's prison will be much less. However, the watchtower will still be heavily guarded. That is the detail I had to leave to her. How to get you in there undetected. I know she'll figure something out."

"I thought you said we don't have to pull the Kill Switch. You found a way for someone else to do it?"

"Yes, we did, but we still need my cartridge placed in the Kill Switch terminal and then taken out before anyone sees. I know you can get in and out through the AC duct, but I don't know how to get everyone, including Neil Elder, out. You'll have a few minutes to load the virus while the systems are rebooting. Even if they caught you, they would never detect the virus. However, if you do get caught, they will torture you. You will eventually break and tell them about our secret weapon. Then the plan will most definitely be lost for good."

"You think she'll find a way?" Jonah asked.

"I know if you and she work together, you will succeed. But don't you worry about that now. You have a year until she comes, and I want you to enjoy this year, not just use up all your time digging. Now, look at this," Matt said, pushing a button on the Portable. The small screen lit up. "Can you read that number?"

Jonah looked at the screen and saw seven random numbers and shook his head. "I wouldn't know how to. I've never counted that high."

Matt gave his mischievous grin. "Those are your money points. They are freely yours. I trust you to finish digging that tunnel and doing the first part of the plan. Once you do that, these points are all yours. You can live however you want with them. Though, for the next year, spend them sparingly and don't go into town much unless you need to buy necessary supplies. You wouldn't want to tip anyone off."

Jonah looked back at the numbers again and his eyes opened wide. "It would take five lifetimes to spend all that."

"You will only have ten to twenty years to spend it. When the second half of my plan succeeds, all money points everywhere will be erased. That's why the second half of my plan can't be rushed. Every detail must be perfect."

CHAPTER 6

Jonah sat on his heels and hunched his long back, digging with a short-handled shovel that he and Mr. Matt bought from the store. He no longer dug down, for his tunnel was now going horizontal with the ground above. Along with the shovel, Mr. Matt also bought him working gloves, new clothes, buckets to carry the soil, binoculars and a lot more food. Digging was easy when your belly was full. In fact, he hadn't been hungry since he came to the cabin.

Jonah kept making his way toward the security fence that lined the property of the factory. Soon he would be on the other side and burrowing toward the eight-foot tunnel the security guard had dug leading from the AC duct under the factory walls. Jonah placed the loose soil into the two buckets behind him. Once they were full, he would bring the buckets to the wheelbarrow just inside the tree line. As he dug, he felt his family's presence just behind him. They kept him company while he tunneled through the earth.

"You know what, Papa? Digging ain't so bad. Mr. Matt has a mirror in the little cabin there. It ain't much bigger than a small window, but I can see my muscles on my shoulders and along my arms. Mr. Matt calls them my triceps. I'm getting strong. Even my legs are getting bigger. I have a feeling that when I turn eighteen, I'll be bigger than you. Since I'm a bodyguard now…it's official. Mr. Matt got me my license and everything using his old-style computer, but it doesn't go into effect until I turn eighteen. Well, since it's official now, I need to be big because I'm supposed to be protecting people." Jonah looked at the dark soil in front of him. A little light from the entrance was still left. Soon, though, the tunnel would be dark, and he would have to work blind. He made his tunnel deep like Mr. Matt suggested, so he wouldn't have to dig through plant roots. He had to purchase a standing flashlight, so he could see where he was digging.

"This soil is way easier to dig in than the dirt we had by the river back home," he continued. "Every time we would put stakes in the ground to build our new huts, we would have to dig through rocks. I ain't seen one rock here. Oh, I forgot. I'm not supposed to say the word *ain't*. Mr. Matt is teaching me to speak Long English correctly. When I'm with him, I always try to talk like he does. He says I'm a quick study. He's taught me a lot of commands on the Portable too with that T-variety. Mamma, I know I already told you, but we have so much money points now in the Portable. We don't ever have to worry about freezing or going hungry again. Maureen and Isaiah will always have full bellies just like mine. Maybe after all this is over, and my year is up, we can go back to the river. I bet most of those pecan trees survived the drought too."

Suddenly, Jonah heard a truck motor coming up from the rocky street that led to the security fence opening. He instantly went into action. He moved the buckets of soil in front of him and crawled backward to the opening of the tunnel. The large rock he created as his own gravestone was next to the entrance. He took the metal tripod laying on the floor of the tunnel and opened it just under the opening. Then he scooted the rock over the hole, carefully allowing the tripod to take some of the weight of the large stone. The stone was large enough to rest on the edges of the ground surrounding the hole, but the tripod added more stability. He would have to wait here until the vehicle made its way into the factory yard and parked next to the watchtower or in one of the garages. After what felt like more than ten minutes, he still heard the hum of the motor. He wondered what was taking so long. Finally, he could hear the voices of two men coming up to the graveyard.

"What do you suppose these are?" a man asked.

"Well, they look like tombstones," another man said. "Let me read here. Jonah Goodman the Second. Then there is Mary Goodman."

The other voice piped in. "I see Isaiah Goodman and Maureen Goodman. What's that big one over there say?"

One of the voices came closer to where Jonah was hiding. "This one is Jonah Goodman the Third. Looks like an entire family was buried here."

"The rumors are true," the other man said. His voice filled with fear.

"What rumors?"

"I heard it when I was at one of the diners in this small village. It was next to a Sleeper factory they had just opened. These workers behind me at another table were talking about how the equipment for the factory came from another factory far away. And there was a mass shooting or some kind of massacre at the factory. They said there were snakes and the people revolted. It sounded too far-fetched to me, but these tombstone markings look fresh."

"That can't be true. We would have heard something on the World News." The other voice sounded skeptical.

"The World News wouldn't mention anything about the Colonials, especially a bunch of them being slaughtered."

"They do it all the time."

"They only report when Colonials kill other Colonials, not Colonials being executed by Security Guards."

"You think it's true?"

"They said all the factory workers died—even the women and children."

"They don't have women and children working in factories!"

"They said this one was different—an experiment of sorts. They said hundreds of people died. Those tombstones prove it. It's an entire family down there. This whole field is probably a graveyard filled with families, but I'm not going to go dig anything up to prove it. It's best to keep our mouths shut."

"Who was the factory director at the time?"

Jonah heard silence. Finally, a voice said, "The one and the same."

"No way. Neil Elder was here then?"

"He's been here a while. They say he's guarding something in the watchtower."

"And what about this women's prison we are supposed to guard? What does he think about that?"

"He doesn't care about a bunch of women pulling cotton. His focus is elsewhere. He worships the World Government, and I think he wants to run our region someday."

"He wants to be a magistrate like Arthur Pallue? I would hate that job. Plus, I'm sure his daughter is in line to take his place."

"Maybe, but she's just a kid. Neil Elder has way more experience. Should we tell him about the tombstones?"

"Hell, no! Are you kidding? If he hasn't said anything yet, we won't. Let's get out of here before someone sees us."

The voices trailed off as the footsteps made their way back to the idled truck.

Jonah hadn't noticed, but his knuckles were pushing against the soil on either side of him into the thick lining of the tunnel. He had to yank his fists out of the holes they created. Soil flung into his face, but he didn't care. Rage filled his body. When the truck finally made its way into one of the garages and the sound of the motor stopped, he knocked the tripod aside and placed the rock onto his shoulder, throwing the boulder over his head with all his strength. It landed several feet past the graves of his family members. He wanted to yell out, but he knew someone would hear him. Finally, he shook his hands and turned to face his father's gravestone. "I promise you, Papa," Jonah whispered coolly, "I will make Neil Elder pay for what he did to our family, and I will take down his precious World Government along with him."

CHAPTER 7

The tremors in Matt's body continued. Jonah placed several blankets over him before he left to dig, but the cold still crept into his bones. He looked toward the window in his room. Though his vision blurred he could see light streaming in through the glass. It was a warm day, but his frail body felt no warmth. He only had a little whiskey left to warm his bones, but he doubted it would do any good now. He was dying, but he felt like his plan was in good hands. Jonah seemed to be doing well. He was a strong young man, and he dug quickly. He was also learning how to be a low-level Efficientist, which was a requirement for bodyguards. Matt had him reading every night. He learned fast. His brain yearned for knowledge. He didn't know what Jonah would do after he completed the first part of his plan, but it would be a waste of his life to go back to living by the river and the pecan trees. There was something special about Jonah Goodman. His life was spared for a reason. Matt quickly turned his head. He heard rustling at the back door. The sound of the wheelbarrow stopped. Matt looked back at the window. It was still too early for Jonah to come back to the cabin. He already had his lunch. He normally dug into the night and ate a late dinner.

Jonah walked into the cabin. He took off his boots outside, but he didn't bother to strip and wash his muddy skin in the water bucket as was customary.

"I hate him!" Jonah yelled after he shut the door behind him.

Matt hoped that Jonah was making progress from the death of his family, but he knew healing would take time. Jonah was close with his family, and grief had a process, which he never bothered to study since he never grieved the loss of anyone—not even his father and mother whom he barely knew.

"Come here, my son," Matt said from his bed.

Jonah walked into his room. Angry tears streaked down his dirty face. His fists were balled by his side.

"Should we have another chat with Christina Straight on the Portable? She's been helping you work through your loss."

"No, I don't want to talk with Miss Christina today. I want to talk to you."

"Can you grab me the last of my whiskey?" Matt asked. He knew he would need his strength to reason with Jonah. He was a respectful young man, but when he set his mind on something, it would be hard to change it. Matt had a suspicion of what Jonah wanted to discuss with him.

A few seconds later, Jonah handed him a small glass with the last of the whiskey. It wasn't much, but it would allow him to get out of bed one last time. He poured the amber liquid into his mouth, savoring the flavor before swallowing. Then he set the glass on the nightstand and turned his attention back to Jonah.

Jonah paced the room. "There has to be a way for me to do both plans. I will do my part in taking down the World Government, but I also want to kill Neil Elder for what he did. He must be held accountable!"

"If you kill him, you will live a life on the run, and that's only if you don't get caught, tortured and killed first. It is a risk. You also risk Christina's life. I still don't know her plans of distracting the guards, so you can place the cartridge in the Kill Switch terminal."

Jonah stopped pacing and said, "Listen to me. I know I promised you that I will do my part. You have given me those money points, and I will not fail you. But you must find a way for me to accomplish both plans. I can't keep digging, knowing that the killer of my family sits up there in the watchtower unaccountable for the crimes he has committed."

Matt carefully pulled one blanket at a time away from his body with shaking hands. "Here, my boy. Help me out of bed. I want to show you something."

Jonah walked to the old man and gently swung his legs over the bed. Then he put his arms around Matt's thin frame and pulled him to his feet.

Matt began to shuffle toward the door of his room. "Follow me."

Jonah followed behind Matt as they made their way through the back door.

"You see this?"

"Yes, but I don't know what it is," Jonah said.

"It's called a refrigerator. It keeps things cool. I'm surprised you never asked about it."

Jonah nodded. "Yes, I remember the guards talking about one. You have a lot of stuff around here that I don't ask about."

Matt smiled. "Jonah, you are about to inherit this cabin, my Portable and everything in it. Except for the old-style computer. That goes to Christina Straight."

Jonah nodded. "Yes, I know. I wouldn't know how to use it anyway."

Matt scratched his chin. "That's not good. She won't know how to use it either. I'm glad you said something. I'll have to teach you the basics tonight, so you can show her."

Jonah nodded. "I will learn."

"Now look down there. I have fuel in a tank located just under us."

"In the ground?"

"Yes, I dug it when I was a much stronger man when I first moved here. I don't know how much fuel is left. I refueled it several months ago. I must add fuel to the generator a few times a week in order to keep the fridge cool and to charge the Portable and computer. The nozzle is there, and the hose connects to the fuel. You'll have to go to the local trading center and get more fuel soon. Now open the fridge. What do you see?"

Jonah leaned down and opened the tiny white box. The shiny weapon caught his eye first. "I see a gun."

The man nodded. "It only has one bullet. I kept it just in case the pain became too much for me. The other thing there is antivenom. I used two vials on you, so there is one left. I always kept it for myself just in case I got bit. Little did I know that God had other plans. But there is something missing."

"What?" Jonah asked. There did seem to be a lot more space than was needed.

"I ran out of my insulin the day I found you. I didn't order more because I was planning to go back to the city and finish the details of the second half of my plan. Interesting, isn't it? I ran out of the very thing keeping me alive the same day I was able to save you."

"Should we get you more?" Jonah asked. "I can take you to the hospital."

"It's too late for me. Once you give my old-style computer to Christina Straight, she will take over the second part of my plan. I'm glad I found her. I don't think I would have lasted more than a few more years even on the insulin. And do not take me to the colonial hospital. They will mark me as dead, and the World Government will confiscate all my money points."

Jonah looked back at the small, opened refrigerator. "Why are you showing me this gun?"

"I'm offering you that bullet. I'm in a lot of pain. I have no insulin and no pain meds. But I'll save myself a quick death, so you can have your revenge. I don't agree with it. I think your life has potential. If you kill him and don't get caught, you will live a life on the run. You can live off the money points, but any value you want to add to this world will be gone."

"I lost my value when I lost my family."

"I greatly disagree. I didn't know your family, but I think they would too. I believe your father and mother would want you to live a life of purpose for good, not give it all away on revenge."

"You know nothing about my family!"

Matt slowly bent over and closed the refrigerator. The young man was understandably troubled and angry. He hoped the sessions with Christina Straight would help, and he knew they were, but these things took time. Recovering from such loss may take years, but deep down in his heart, Matt believed that Jonah would recover. However, the act of taking someone's life was an entirely different trauma that Jonah would have to deal with for the rest of his life.

He turned to the young man and placed a hand on his shoulder. "I have never had children, so I don't know what it feels like to love and care for someone. But ever since I found you, my life has been fuller. And I feel like I'm imparting something greater to this world than I ever did producing in the city. To me, you are my greatest accomplishment. I place great value in our relationship. I know my words won't take away the hurt you feel, but you have given me a greater sense of purpose than I have ever experienced. Whether you finish your part of the plan or not, I am honored to know you, Jonah Goodman the Third. I sense a lot of greatness in you."

Jonah said nothing, but Matt could see the tears forming in his eyes. This moment, his words, are what T-variety could never accomplish. Only language rich with emotions could sway a man's life one way or another. Matt's mind was instantly drawn to Eve Pallue, the daughter of Arthur Pallue. He wondered if she would wind up like half the kids at the Learning Life Centers—detached, depressed and a social outcast—or would she overcome a life of solitude and achieve something great?

Matt finally exhaled. His body ached all over. "Listen, just like I entrusted you with the money points, I will trust you to make the right decisions about Neil Elder. The gun and bullet are yours. Just promise me one thing."

"What?" Jonah whispered.

"If you do plan on killing him, do it after Christina Straight is released from prison. She will be there six months. Let her leave and get the old-style computer back to the city. Don't do it when the Kill Switch is being pulled. Don't compromise the plan for this revenge of yours. Then after six months, you can go through your tunnel and shoot Neil Elder for killing your family. And plan your escape. Purchase a vehicle. Have a place to go. Be smart about it. Don't just go in there in blind rage. I want you to make it out. Will you promise me that?"

Jonah thought a moment finally giving a hesitant nod.

"Is that a yes?"

"Yes."

"Good. Now help me back to bed."

Jonah led Matt back into the cabin. He picked him up and placed him in his bed, covering him with every blanket available.

"Do you want me to buy you more whiskey?" Jonah asked. "Are you hungry? Do you want some soup, or would you like some water?"

Matt shook his head. "No. I just need rest. Why don't you give Christina Straight a call in a little while? I can tell she enjoys her chats with you."

"I may," Jonah said. "I'm going back out to continue my dig for a while."

"Good idea. The exercise will help you clear your head."

Jonah took several steps toward the door before Matt called to him.

"Jonah, if anything happens to me, don't bury me in that field. Bury me near the cabin. And I don't want a gravestone. Just plant something over my grave. Something beautiful that will benefit from the nutrients of my decaying body."

"Have you made your peace with God?" Jonah asked.

Matt heard tenderness in Jonah's voice. He could tell the boy cared for him, and he hated that he had to add another name to his list of losses.

"Yes, I've read much of the Apostle's writings. I even started reading the Gospels of the New Testament. Things are making more sense now. I guess that happens once your time on earth is ending," Matt said with a laugh. "I plan on having a chat with Him now. I need to ask a few more questions before I commit."

Jonah smiled. "I've got some digging to do. I have a little over nine months to reach the factory."

"You are strong," Matt said with pride. "And you work hard. If I ever had a son, I would want him to be like you."

Jonah said nothing but gave a slight nod. He turned and walked through the bedroom door, closing it gently behind him. As he left, Matt knew that would be the last time he would see the young man. And for the first time he prayed.

"God, it's me, Matthew Coughlin. I know I ignored You all my life. You can't blame me because I didn't know much about You, but I'm ready to have that Gift You said is mine for free. That Son of Yours, Jesus, He lived a perfect life, and You said He will give it to me in exchange for my mess of a life. I know Heaven is where You are, and if You are love, that's where I want to be. I accept Your Son Jesus as my Lord and Savior. Now I can have Your Spirit, the Holy Spirit, with me now, so I can have You with me when this frail body dies tonight."

Matt experienced a warmth pour over his body from his head to his toes. It felt like a large jar of oil being emptied over him.

"Wow," he whispered. "That feels amazing. If this is what heaven feels like, I want it."

The trembling in Matt's body calmed, and a peace flooded the inside space of him that had always searched and striven. His eyelids dropped, and his breathing slowed. He couldn't help but smile. The thing he feared most in life had become the most wonderful experience of his life.

"And one more thing since You're obviously listening to me," Matt said, opening his eyes. "Help Jonah. I truly care for him. He needs guidance while he's alone. Make sure he keeps in constant contact with Christina Straight. And help him to not take his revenge. I think if he kills Neil Elder, it will eat him up inside over the years. He's such a good, innocent young man. I don't want him to change. Thank You for listening. I'm ready now to leave this old body. The two parts of my plan are set and in capable hands. The rest is up to You."

As Matthew Coughlin drifted off to eternal sleep, a flock of white doves skirted the trees of the forest and descended to perch on the roof of the small cabin. Their cooing sounds combined together to make a bittersweet song of Matt's passing.

CHAPTER 8

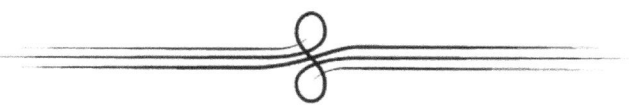

Jonah placed the long-handled shovel against the wall and went back to the gravesite to inspect his work. He left a large cavity in the middle of the grave about three feet deep and three feet wide. He couldn't help but smile. This year he had become an expert at digging.

"May you rest in peace, Matthew Coughlin. Though we were not related, I consider you like an uncle to me. That is what I will call you. Uncle Matt instead of Mr. Matt. I promise to speak Long English correctly. I promise to fulfill the first part of your plan. And—my other plan." He paused and cleared his throat. "Now, Uncle Matt, Miss Christina asked that I contact her on the Portable when I finished. I have something to show her."

Jonah walked back to the cabin door and washed his hands in the bucket of fresh water from the creek. He dried them with the towel hanging over the doorknob and pushed the door open. Once in the cabin, he picked up the Portable from the table. Every time he put his thumb to the print identifier and the screen glowed, it gave Jonah a sense of achievement. He owned a Portable. He owned money points. He was a free man. He used the T-variety commands that Uncle Matt had taught him. "Visual Call. Christina Straight." Then he grabbed one of the chairs by the table and dragged it outside with him.

A moment later, Miss Christina's face appeared on the screen. "Good morning, Miss Christina." Jonah said, setting the chair next to the freshly tilled soil. Christina had pale skin and a thin face with hazel eyes and light brown hair. To him, she looked to be in her late twenties, but she said she was thirty-eight, which was his mother's age. At first, he felt uncomfortable talking with her through the Portable, but now he was used to it. She had a way of making him feel comfortable and understood.

"Well, good morning to you, Jonah," she said, smiling.

He liked it when she smiled. She was always in a good mood, and Jonah could tell she enjoyed their chats. "I've buried Mr. Matt, and I decided to call him Uncle Matt if that is okay."

"I think it is very fitting," she affirmed.

"I have a surprise for you, so I'm going to set the Portable down on this chair facing the grave."

"Sounds good."

He pulled the Portable stand down and set it on the chair facing the freshly tilled earth. "Uncle Matt wanted me to plant something over his grave, so I went to a plant nursery and bought two plants. It was expensive, but I know he would love it."

"I'm sure he will," her voice rang out from the Portable.

"Just wait for one second while I get it," Jonah said. He walked behind the grave and gripped a large tree sapling about four feet tall. He brought it back into view of the Portable. "This is a Caddo Pecan Tree sapling," he said, confidently. "It must have another mate in order to cross pollinate, so I already planted an Elliot Pecan Tree fifty feet over there," he said pointing away from the Portable. "That way both trees can produce pecans. I am planting this one over Uncle Matt's grave because he didn't want a gravestone. Instead, he asked for something beautiful, and I can't think of anything better than a pecan tree."

Jonah looked at the Portable screen and waited for Miss Christina's expression. Her already pleasant countenance turned into wonderment.

"Jonah, I believe Matthew would love that. He knows those trees are a sweet memory from your childhood."

Jonah nodded. "Would you like to watch me plant it? Then you can offer some words."

"Yes, I would love that."

Jonah took the tree sapling and placed it into the cavity he created over Matt's grave. Then he walked to the wheelbarrow filled with fresh soil. He wheeled it next to the grave and carefully scooped handfuls of soil around the sapling, packing the soil down as he went. Once the cavity was filled, he moved the wheelbarrow away and dusted his hands off on his jeans. "There, Miss Christina. Now all we must do is wait. The trees will start producing in a few years, but it will take about ten to twelve years for the trees to yield a big harvest. At least, that is what the store owner told me."

"Do not despise small beginnings, for the Lord rejoices to see the work begin," Christina said.

"I like that, Miss Christina. Is that another one of your Bible verses?"

"Yes, it is. It comes from Zechariah 4:10. It means that sometimes God's greatest moves start with the tiniest of plans. It reminds me of Matthew Coughlin. He had a plan, and you and I will do our part. I have prayed on it, and I know that God is with me. I don't understand it all yet, but I am to do what I can and leave the rest in His hands. And like these trees, once you and I plant our part, we will have to wait years to see the harvest. But in my heart, I believe the harvest will be the freedom of many souls. And tragedies like what happened to your family will finally come to an end."

Jonah said nothing, but he felt a sting in his eyes. He didn't want to cry. Miss Christina had seen enough of his tears.

"Do you still talk with your family while you dig?" she asked.

He nodded. "It makes me feel good. And now I can talk to Uncle Matt when I'm home."

"And I'm here too whenever you need me. In fact, you are the only name I allow to call me at any time day or night on my Portable."

"Thank you, Miss Christina. Would you like to say a few words for Uncle Matt before I go? I need to get back to my tunnel. I'm almost to the fence. I want to get to the factory wall ahead of schedule, so I don't have to worry about not reaching you in time."

"I would be honored," she said.

She closed her eyes, so Jonah closed his.

"Dear Father, thank You for allowing us to meet this dear servant of yours, Matthew Coughlin. I believe he had a heart change before he died, so I know I will see him one day when I get to sit in Your glory. Thank You for allowing me to write words that change hearts. Thank You for Jonah who can work so hard as he carries the burden of so much pain. I pray dear God that the hurt of his great loss would be gently lifted from him, and that his sorrow will be turned to gladness. Thank You most of all for Your Son, Jesus, who left His glory, so He could walk in the shadows of our pain with us. We are never alone. I pray this in Your Name, amen."

"Amen," Jonah said. Miss Christina's words both moved and agitated him. He hoped she couldn't read his mood, which she often did. She could always tell how he was feeling. "Thank you for the prayer. I best be going. I have a tunnel to dig."

"Okay, Jonah. Remember, call me anytime."

Jonah picked up the Portable from the chair. "Yes, ma'am. I will."

"Bye, Jonah."

"Bye, Miss Christina."

Christina Straight's face disappeared, and Jonah turned off the Portable. He stared at his reflection in the dark screen. "I know what I'm planning is wrong, God. But that gun and bullet were left there for a reason. I will do my part, but once Miss Christina goes back to the city, I will sneak into the factory and shoot Neil Elder in his sleep. I already bought a mask. No one will know it's me. Then I can stay in my cabin near my family and live in peace."

Christina needed to get work done, but she couldn't help thinking about Jonah. He was not yet eighteen years old and would be alone for almost nine months. She wanted to intervene somehow, but she felt God telling her to let him be. He needed that time alone—though, she would insist on their weekly chats. Matthew Coughlin confided to her before he died that he had given Jonah a gun and a bullet. He didn't want to, but Jonah left him no choice. However, she reminded Matt that Jonah could easily purchase both with the money points he was leaving him. At least this way, if he went through with killing Neil Elder, there would be less evidence pointed at him because he never made a gun purchase.

"Come on, Christina. You have nine months to finish your caseload, complete six months of faith writings and figure out a way to attack the World News," she said to herself.

She had read the second part of Matthew Coughlin's plan. It was ingenious, but she needed to find a way to make Arthur Pallue command Neil Elder to pull the Kill Switch. The second part of the plan all hinged on the Kill Switch being pulled. From what Matthew had described, the Kill Switch was protected by an encasement and needed keys to open. The security guard he was working with previously could have opened and pulled the switch, but he died. That's why she needed to attack the World News. It was the most vulnerable of all the World Government's systems. She wished she could get her hands on that old-style computer Matt told her about. They discussed sending it to her, but they couldn't get the Runners involved. They worked for the World Government running items to homes and businesses, and they were known as gossips. The less people who knew Jonah was in that cabin the better. She would keep with the original plan. Once she finished creating the attacks, she would send them to Jonah's Portable. Then, with the tunnel finished, they would find a time to meet up and dispense the attacks via the computer.

"But how can I attack them?" she whispered, turning her wheeled chair in a circle. She loved looking at her home. She kept her LPS against the wall in the living room. Although she lived in the city, her condo was the ground floor away from the high-rises. Colorful décor adorned every room in her condo, and she filled any space she could with live plants. Most Efficientists thought her decorating was a waste of time, but she knew better. A place of beauty could heal and empower the soul. She had already hired a retired Mother who was now a caretaker of Efficientists' homes to stay in her home for the six months while she was in prison.

"Prison," she whispered. Chills swept across her body. She was not looking forward to going—all because she wouldn't disclose information about one of her patients.

"That's it!" she shouted and stood up. "I don't need to attack the World News. I need the World News to attack Arthur Pallue, and I know plenty of people who have dirt on him. I'll feed the World News the information, and he'll have to shut the systems down!"

She sat back into her chair and swiveled around to face her LPS screen. It was time to contact all her troops. She had almost a thousand people in her growing army that the World News amply named the Efficientists Christian Sect. She would get as much documented defaming information on Arthur Pallue as she could and leak it through the World News once she got onto the old-style computer. Matthew Coughlin said that she could go anywhere and do anything undetected on the computer, so the World News wouldn't be able to stop the flow of information even if they wanted to try as they may. After a few minutes of hearing and seeing all the embarrassing information she gathered on him, Arthur Pallue would demand Neil Elder pull the Kill Switch.

CHAPTER 9

Jonah liked the look of the fields of white cotton puffing out of their shells. The normally green plants gleamed white like the snow he always heard about but had never seen. Even during the freeze when he was young, it didn't snow. But he read about snow and looked at the photos on his Portable. He wondered why the World Government had hired Colonials to plant the cotton. Maybe they knew that the labor they would receive from the imprisoned Efficientists wouldn't be so efficient. He doubted the women's prison would last long. Matt Coughlin may have initiated the change on his old-style computer, but once the prison become unproductive, the chain of command would be scrutinized. Look as they may, they would find the orders but not who originally sent them. Jonah just hoped that the scrutiny wouldn't happen until after he and Christina Straight completed their parts of Uncle Matt's plan.

Uncle Matt would be proud of him. He had been doing a lot of reading on his Portable. He was learning so much. In fact, he never realized that he would love studying history, cultures, sciences—he especially enjoyed studying maps. He looked at maps of both the cities and Colonies. He would study a village's map before he drove there. He even studied the city where Christina Straight lived. He could see her ground floor condo on the maps. She was quite impressed with how much he was learning. His mamma and papa would be so impressed with him too. Jonah looked back at the road. He hadn't visited their gravesite in a while since he finished the tunnel. He had snuck around in the factory a few times, but it only left him with bad memories. Instead, he bought a fancy, black SUV and drove from town to town during the day, making sure he came back home to his cabin each night. He still had a part of a plan to finish.

He stopped visiting the village closest to him. The town's people started asking too many questions, and people began recognizing him more. Instead, he would go into villages twenty to a hundred miles away. He would eat at one of their diners and do a little shopping, but he never spent too much. Fuel stations usually took money points. He would buy extra fuel because most people would give anything for a gallon of it. Fuel was great for bartering with people who didn't take money points. That's how he bought his SUV. He was at a fuel station about ten miles away. He had to walk there to get gas for his generator and for bartering. The store owner noticed that he had a Portable and asked where his vehicle was. Jonah lied and said he had no interest in buying one. He liked walking. It was good exercise.

That's when the owner broke down crying. He said he had an SUV for sale. He bought it for his son as a present just before he died. He hoped seeing the shiny vehicle would spur his son's spirits to fight his sickness, but his son had no interest in driving. He died only a few weeks later in a Colonial hospital. The doctors said that nothing could be done. He didn't want the SUV in his parking lot one more day. It was a constant reminder that his son was gone. He told Jonah he bought it for 7500 money points, but he would sell it to him for 5000. The transaction was made, and the man gave him a quick lesson on driving. That day changed his life. He loved driving. It reminded him of how truly free he was.

As he got closer to the turn off for the factory, he slowed his SUV. He never parked it near his cabin. He built a large hut—one like he used to make when he was little sleeping near the pecan trees—but this one was several times bigger. It became his garage, hiding his vehicle. Then it was about a fifteen-minute walk back to his cabin. He carefully turned into the forest, finding the path he had created. He had to be very careful of the tree stumps. He hit one once and had to replace a tire. Once he finally made it to the large hut, he put his SUV in park. He got out and moved the large panel made up of branches away from the front of the hut. Then he got back into his SUV and gently pulled inside. Once he turned off the motor, he got out, opened the back and got the two boxes of food and other supplies he had bought. Finally, he put the wooden panel back, concealing his SUV once again.

As he walked back to his cabin, he couldn't help but whistle. It had been a good day. He woke up and did his work out. Instead of digging these days, he started a collection of dumbbells, bars and plates. They were old and beat up, but he would lift them. He liked his large physique, and he wanted to keep it. He noticed men would move out of his way when he walked down the streets of the villages. He no longer felt like a boy. He was now a man. His eighteenth birthday was not too far off. He thought of Uncle Matt. He said he could be his bodyguard in the city once he turned eighteen, but instead he gave him all his money points before he died. Jonah wondered which one he would want more—money points and a life of ease or to be a bodyguard with a life of purpose?

Abruptly, Jonah stopped whistling. He heard hums of truck motors—several of them. He ran to the forest line that rimmed the road and hid behind a large tree. As the trucks passed, he looked at one of them. They were security vans. The prisoners were here, and Christina Straight was in one of them. Jonah ran back into the forest toward his cabin. He was supposed to be available every day in the AC duct. She would try to make it to him as soon as she could. He had already sent her the image of the map of the factory, so she knew exactly where he would be hiding. They needed to meet to arrange their plan. Christina wanted to implement their parts of the plan quickly, so Jonah would no longer be in danger of being found out. She was worried that with more security detail at the factory, he would soon be discovered. She wanted him safe. She also believed she found a way to get him into the watchtower after the Kill Switch was pulled without detection, but she needed to test the old-style computer first.

When Jonah made it to his cabin, he unlocked the backdoor. He had added several locks and deadbolts since he first moved there, so it took a little more time. No one had ever bothered him at the cabin, but he wanted to be more careful. He was protecting a Portable with millions of money points and an old-style computer with a plan to take down the World Government. He was not yet eighteen and protector of so much.

"Don't despise small beginnings," he mused. "Or young people." Once he closed the door behind him, he set his two boxes down. He needed to get to the tunnel. His heart rate accelerated. He had been waiting for this moment for a year, and he couldn't believe it was finally here. He left his cabin, making sure to secure the back door again. He crept quickly through the trees. He could walk the path to his tunnel with his eyes closed. He had walked the same path several times a day for a year. Once he got close to the field, he saw the trucks in the factory yard. Women were being led out of trucks and in through the front doors. There were around ten trucks, so probably about sixty women. He ducked and headed back to his tunnel. He needed to get in place just in case she was able to get to him early.

Right as he was about to roll the stone that marked his grave, he heard a woman scream. Then gunshots. He ran back to where he could see the trucks.

"It's a rattlesnake! Kill it! Kill it!"

Gun fire rang out, but it was not directed at the women. It was directed at the ground in front of the security vans. Jonah's heart raced. He had to get closer to see if someone was bit. He had heard a women scream. The voice sounded familiar. "No, it can't be her. Oh God, not Miss Christina," he whispered desperately.

He crawled along the fence until he could hear the security guards talking.

"You can stop shooting now. The snake is dead."

"Was it really a rattlesnake?"

Jonah had to concentrate to hear. The sounds of women weeping made it difficult to discern the security guards' words.

"She's been bitten," a woman cried out. "You can see the bite marks on the back of her ankle!"

"What is going on here?" a voice demanded.

Jonah looked up and saw a man holding a Portable in one hand. It was Neil Elder.

A female security guard walked back holding two pieces of a snake. "This rattlesnake bit her, but we took care of it."

"You were supposed to make sure that the basement was clear of snakes!" Neil yelled to the lead guard.

"We did. This one came from the fields."

Neil waved his free arm. "It's like this place is cursed. Who is the victim? Is she high ranking?"

Another security guard answered. "Her name is Christian Straight. Yes, she is high ranking."

"Damn it!" Neil yelled, kicking the dirt. "She cannot die. I told them that making this factory into a prison was a stupid idea. She shouldn't even be here. I will have whoever's head for this ridiculous order!"

Jonah knew that Christina Straight had a contingency plan to make it out of prison alive, especially now that she would be seeing Neil Elder again. She had sent classified information of one of their counseling sessions where he admitted that he wanted Eve Pallue dead. Neil Elder would do everything possible to keep Christina Straight alive.

"What should we do?" the female security guard asked.

"Take her to the hospital. Now!" Neil screamed.

"But sir, I don't think Colonial hospitals have antivenom. It's too expensive," she said.

"Then take her back to the city! Do what you need to do!"

"That's an eight-hour drive. She won't make it," the lead security guard interjected.

Neil grabbed the security guard's shirt and pulled his face to his own. "Then you better pray that the Colonial doctor on call has other means of saving this woman's life because if she dies, so do you!"

"Yes, sir!" the man shouted.

Neil threw the man aside. "Now get her into the van and to the hospital! I'll call the doctor personally and demand she live."

Jonah instantly went into action. He crawled away from the fence, and once he got to the forest, he ran faster than he had ever run before. It had gotten dark outside, but he sprinted back to his cabin without a single misstep. Finally, he fell in front of the refrigerator next to his cabin and opened it. The gun was now safely inside his nightstand, but he kept the vial of antivenom in the fridge along with milk and a few other perishables.

He stood up and looked toward the grave where the pecan tree he had planted had now grown twice its size. "Thank you, Uncle Matt, for suggesting I keep it."

Then he grabbed the handcloth he kept on top of the fridge and wrapped it around the vial. He didn't have a needle, but the hospital would. He stood up and shoved the towel and antivenom into his pocket. Then he patted his other pocket to ensure his car keys were there. Now he needed to get to his SUV and drive to the hospital. Somehow, he would get the vial of antivenom to the doctor. He needed to get there before the security van did, though. Instantly, Jonah took off running. He would make sure that Miss Christina would not die. He would protect her.

"I will do my best," Doctor Prator said, turning off her Portable. The man on the other end was adamant. She fidgeted with the stethoscope around her neck. She pulled her grey-streaked red hair behind her collar. "The World Government cannot demand that I save someone's life, especially someone with a rattlesnake bite," she said to herself. She had heard rumors about Neil Elder, the Efficientist who ran the factory just outside of town. To be on his bad side would be detrimental if not fatal. She explained to him that she had treated rattlesnake bites before and the survival rate was fifty/fifty, but he insisted that this woman, Christina Straight, live. Then he threatened to have her medical license revoked.

"I hope she's healthy," she whispered. "Otherwise, she won't have the energy to fight for her life. She'll find no antivenom at a Colonial hospital."

Suddenly, the door of her office crashed opened. She stood to her feet. The largest black youth she had ever seen faced her. He was sweating profusely and out of breath.

"I tried to stop him," a man in blue scrubs said, coming from behind him.

"I know they are sending you a woman named Christina Straight!" the young man yelled.

She crossed her arms. "My patients are confidential. You must leave this room now, or I will call security!"

"I already called them, Doctor Prator. They should be here any minute."

"Please listen to me," the young man spoke quieter. "I have antivenom. I was there when she was bit. I was hiding behind the fence because I heard noises."

"How do you have antivenom?" she asked, skeptically.

"I was bitten a year ago twice by a rattlesnake, and my uncle—he's from the city—he administered it to me. I kept the other vial in a fridge that I keep on a generator. I just want to help. Please, let me reach into my pocket. I have it here."

She stared at the young man. After years of working at a Colonial hospital, she had excellent discernment. He was telling the truth.

"Okay, let me see it," she said.

"Please call off security. I can't be seen. If the security guards know I was sneaking by the factory, they'll kill me."

Doctor Prator thought of her talk with the factory director, Neil Elder. She wouldn't put it past him to kill a young man for eavesdropping.

"John, please shut the door and call off security. Don't let anyone know what has happened here. People's lives are at stake right now. I'll explain it all to you later."

The nurse wavered, but he finally nodded his head. "Yes, Doctor. I'll be right outside if you need me." He closed the door behind him.

"Thank you," she said and walked up to the youth. "Let me see it."

Jonah reached into his pocket and pulled out the washcloth. Then he carefully unwrapped the vial and presented it to the doctor.

"It's still cold," she whispered.

"Please make sure Christina Straight gets it. She is a very important Efficientist."

"Neil Elder told me," she said.

The youth's face hardened. "And he is a very bad man. Tell him nothing. He is not to be trusted."

"But he sure wants this Christina Straight to be saved," she said. "In fact, he demanded it."

"Believe me. If he does, it is for selfish reasons. He's ruthless. The less you tell him, the safer you will be."

"You're pretty smart for your age," she said. "And brave."

"I must go now. Please, that vial is for Miss Christina."

"I'll make sure it goes to her," the doctor answered. She watched the young man as he opened the door and walked past the nurse.

"Everything okay?" John asked.

"Here," she said, handing the vial to the nurse. "This is antivenom. Get it prepped. The patient should be here soon."

"Yes, Doctor."

"And John. Let me do the talking. That woman is coming from the factory run by Neil Elder. Supposedly, it is now a prison for women Efficientists. We don't want Mr. Elder or any of his guards asking questions. Silence is crucial. And that young man. We never saw him."

"Understood," the nurse said and left the room.

Doctor Prator stood a moment longer, thinking. The young man had called the patient *Miss Christina*, like he knew her. She could see it in his eyes. She had seen the same look in every person who had a loved one in the hospital. It was a desperation of love. The doctor knew there was more to his story than he was letting on, but it would be one she would soon forget. Patient confidentiality had created in her mind a place where she put information and locked it away for good. The young man was correct. The less you said, the safer you would be.

CHAPTER 10

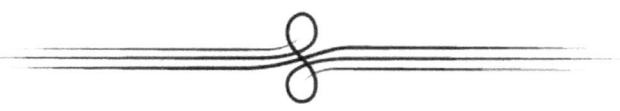

N eil Elder sat at his desk high in the watchtower. He had just sent his request to be transferred. It was time for him to go back to the city. The Kill Switch could add nothing more to his rank—unless, of course he could actually use it. However, Arthur Pallue would not allow it to be tested. Why would he? Erasing all the systems of the World Government in hopes they would reboot didn't sound great to him either. He personally had a lot of money points and was on the verge of becoming an Elite Efficientists. He didn't want any of his files to be lost in the reboot. Plus, none of the other regions of the World Government knew about it, but that was Arthur Pallue's department. He was probably keeping it secret to have the upper hand. Being intensely paranoid, he trusted no one.

Neil stood up and walked to the window. Efficientists prisoners were picking through cotton. This whole prison was a joke. He had also sent in a request that the prison be changed back to a prison for Colonial workers who would actually be productive in the cotton fields. He was already over budget, having to hire locals to help with the workload. He tried to find who sent the initial orders to have his factory become a prison, but his search only led to dead ends. It seemed as though everyone received the orders, but no one sent them. He needed to dump this entire factory into another Efficientist's hands, a person eager to take on the project. He turned when he heard the knock on the door.

"Enter," he commanded.

His lead security guard, Officer Evans, brought in the prisoner. "You can leave us, Officer."

Officer Evans nodded and shut the door behind him.

Christina Straight was a tall woman. He would not go near her because their height difference would be too apparent. "So, you are here only for a minute and you try to sabotage me. If we don't work together, we will not make it through the next six months of your sentence."

"You know very well I was not intending to have a rattlesnake bite my leg," she said matter-of-factly. "It was hardly a pleasant welcome to prison."

"The doctor said you are one lucky lady," he said, walking back to his desk and sitting on the corner of the tabletop. "The Colonial hospital just so happened to get a vial of antivenom sent to them by mistake."

"I don't believe in accidents."

"Yes, I know. It's your God," Neil said, pointing up. "He made sure to have it there ready for the day you arrived."

Christina said nothing.

Neil exhaled and stood back up. "Look, you have secrets on me. I have secrets on you. Let's just bury the past and move forward. I will make your time comfortable here, and then we will both return to the city once these six months are over. You can continue helping broken Efficientists one sad story at a time, and I will return to my research."

"You are leaving the factory?" she asked.

Neil quickly glanced at the red Kill Switch against the far wall. "Yes. There is nothing more for me here, but don't worry. I'll be an Elite Efficientist by then, so we will be running in different circles at PR events. You have a high enough rank, but you lack drive."

"My motivation comes from another source other than mere production," she said simply.

"Fine. Have it your way. I just wanted to make sure that you know I did not plant a rattlesnake in the factory yard to attack you. I ensured you were rushed to the hospital and cared for. You survived. There was antivenom. I am not at fault here. I will make sure you leave after your six months, and you can stop that information about me from being spread. I'd send you home now if I could, but we are both stuck in this preposterous situation. If you or any of the other prisoners need anything, just ask Officer Evans. You won't be seeing me. I have work to do before I go back to the city. Questions?"

"Why are there no jail cells? Isn't this a prison?"

Neil tilted his head back and laughed. "Now that is the funniest thing I've heard in a while. A bunch of women Efficientists trying to bust out of prison located in Colonial territory far from every comfort of the city. You all wouldn't last the night out there. I'm not worried about you leaving." He spread out his arms. "Feel free to walk around. Get snacks from the kitchen at night. Walk the grounds inside the fence. Once the workday is done, the rest of the time is yours. I'm sure you'll find your evenings here boring and uneventful."

"Can I have a Portable?"

"Absolutely not. Those are for Efficientists, and right now you are a prisoner. Anything else?"

"I'm finished," she said.

"Good. Now off you go. Maybe you can offer free therapy to the other Efficientists out there. I'm sure being idle will be a new experience for most of them; though, from their records, few of them have high ranks." Neil pulled out the chair under his desk and sat down. Then he turned on his LPS. He wanted to get his research teams ready. He began his clicking on the keyboard and giving short commands. He didn't notice Christina Straight looking at the Kill Switch and the AC duct just above it before she left the room.

Christina quietly walked the halls of the factory. Neil Elder
had been honest. All the security guards were up in their
barracks. She could hear yelling and laughter. The other
prisoners explained to her the day she came back from the
hospital that they would take bottles of liquor to their
rooms and drink all night—so much so that they woke up
late in the morning. This prison really was a joke, but it
worked to her advantage. She worried more about the other
women seeing her than the security guards.

She stopped at the large AC duct on the floor of the
factory hall. She had memorized the plans of the factory
and where the tunnel was located. She looked left and right
to make sure no one was looking. Then she crouched down
and pulled the vent from the wall and slid it away from the
cavity. She threw in her overnight bag. Jonah explained
that her clothes would become soiled as she crawled
through the tunnel, so she should leave an extra pair in the
vent for her to change into when she returned. Finally, she
shimmied into the hole and slid the vent cover back over
the entrance.

She hated confined spaces, but she continued to
make her way down the vent. She crawled through another
opening and into a tunnel through the earth. The tunnel was
much wider than the AC vent. She knew the tunnel was
long, but finally crawling in it gave her a vast appreciation
for how hard Jonah had worked. He had even finished the
tunnel almost two months early. The light in the tunnel
completely disappeared, but she noticed a flashing light in
the distance. It was Jonah. He was at the other entrance of
the tunnel waiting for her. He knew she wanted to meet him
right away. He must have seen the security van return her
from the hospital. It was Jonah who brought the antivenom

to the hospital. Doctor Prator wouldn't admit it, but she gave a knowing look. They were both medical doctors—one for the body and one for the mind. They had to keep their secrets.

The light in the distance still felt so far away. She noticed her breathing had become rapid, and she was feeling lightheaded. She stopped crawling. "Calm down, Christina. Slow your breathing. Jonah spent ten months in this tunnel. You can spend ten minutes in it. Just take one step at a time." She continued to crawl. She thought of her condo in the city with its colorful adornments and lush plants. She imagined watering each plant and whispering sweet nothings to them. Finally, the light was just above her and she stood up. The air of the forest was refreshing compared to the dank smell of the prison. A hand reached out to her.

"Here, Miss Christina. Take my hand and I'll pull you up."

She grabbed his hand, ready to pull herself up with it, but instead, she felt her entire body lifted and placed onto the ground. She looked up at the young man's face. "Wow! I didn't know you were such a big guy."

He let go of her hand and laughed. "I get that a lot. The Goodman family men were always very big, but I think I've outgrown them all." Jonah handed the flashlight to her. "Will you shine that down the entrance? I need to set up the tripod."

"Of course," she said, taking the large flashlight and pointing it down. Jonah crawled on the ground and reached into the entrance to the tunnel with the tripod, setting out the three legs. Then he got up and picked up the large stone and placed it gently over the hole. Christina let the light rest on the stone and read the inscription. "This is your *freedom grave.*"

"Yes," he nodded and extended his hand for the flashlight. "I'll introduce you to my family." He brought the light onto the first gravestone. "This is my papa, Jonah Goodman the Second. This is my mamma, Mary Goodman. This is my brother Isaiah and my sister Maureen. Everyone, this here is Miss Christina. She is going to help me finish the next part of Uncle Matt's plan."

Christina felt a pain in her spirit. The young man was still hurting, and he was coping by talking to his deceased loved ones. It was a common occurrence and nothing to fear, but it meant he continued to grieve. She clasped his free hand and squeezed it. "I am so sorry about the loss of your family."

He looked away. "This is the first time I've come to visit them in a while. I feel ashamed. I don't want them to think I have forgotten them."

Christina took a step closer to the young man. He was big, but he was still just a youth. She wrapped him into her arms. "Jonah, they know you love them. You carry them in your heart, not the grave. They will always be with you. There is no shame in finding happiness after loss. In fact, from what you told me about them, they were truly good parents. They would want you to find joy and peace in life."

She felt Jonah's body begin to tremble.

"I miss them so much, Miss Christina. The hurt I feel goes away sometimes, but then it hits me, and I get so angry. The man who killed them is just over there in that watchtower, and I imagine crawling into the room where he hides and shooting him. All I need is one shot. I read all about how to use my gun, and I've practiced. I went there once, into the watchtower through the vents, and just watched him. He works on his LPS like he has done nothing wrong."

"Jonah, I've said it before. Killing him won't take away the pain."

"Will it take away the anger?" he asked.

"Maybe, but the anger will be replaced with bitterness, guilt and numerous other negative feelings. It will not be replaced with peace."

"I've studied history. Men and women have had to kill all the time during wartime," Jonah said, pulling away from her embrace.

"Yes, but this is not war. This is revenge. Two motives to the same action make that one action two completely different things. But even soldiers during wartime must deal with remorse."

Jonah wiped his face. "We better get to the cabin. I know there is work you need to do."

"Yes, you are right. I want to finally get my hands on that old-style computer. Lead the way."

She carefully walked behind Jonah. She noticed that he didn't look at the ground below him. He must have this trek memorized. She wouldn't say any more about his plan to kill Neil Elder unless he offered to discuss it. He would have to make his own decision. If she made it for him, he would never learn or grow. At least Matthew Coughlin had warned Jonah to wait until her six months were over. Otherwise, he would jeopardize the rest of the plan. She wouldn't mention to Jonah that Neil Elder was planning to leave in six months as well. Maybe the young man would miss his opportunity.

When they finally got to the cabin, she was impressed. It was small but in good condition. As Jonah unlocked the many bolts, she looked to the left. "Is that Matthew's pecan tree?" she asked pointing.

"Yes," he said, looking over his shoulder. "Uncle Matt, we are here. Christina finally made it. We are going to finish the next part of the plan. You have it all ready?"

"Yes, it's all prepared. I sent everything to your Portable. I just need to figure out how to use the old computer to get into it."

"From what Uncle Matt said, it should be simple." Jonah opened the door and waved Christina in. "Welcome to my home."

"Why do you have so many lamps?" she asked, amazed at how well lit the cabin was.

"They are all battery operated. I like to read at night, so I had to buy several of them." He pointed to the desk. "There is the Portable and the old-style computer—both charged and ready."

Christina quickly walked to the chair and sat. She placed her fingers over the keyboard and began to type. "Matthew sent me all the information on how to use it."

Jonah grabbed a chair from the table and slid it to where she was working. "How long will it take? Do you need a few days?"

She continued to type. "We don't have a few days. This must happen tomorrow night. Thank God you saved the antivenom for me and got it to the hospital in time or else I would still be there or worse dead, and we would have missed this chance." She stopped. "Thank you for saving my life by the way. How did you beat the security guards there?"

"You're welcome," he said, smiling. "I own my very own black SUV, and it drives very fast. I keep it hidden in the forest."

"You never cease to amaze me," she said, shaking her head in awe. "Now, I'm in your Portable getting the writings I've done as the Apostle. I'm timing their publication on different sites for the next six months." Relief flooded her chest. "Good. Now I won't be found out. Next, I must get Arthur Pallue to order Neil Elder to pull the Kill Switch."

"How do you plan on doing that?"

"Arthur Pallue is having a PR event for his daughter's eighteenth birthday tomorrow. The World News will be there in droves."

"I'm turning eighteen in a few weeks too," Jonah said intrigued. "I can't believe I'm the same age as Arthur Pallue's daughter."

"She has accomplished a lot in her short eighteen years. She's following right along her father's productive footsteps." She stopped and looked at Jonah. "But I believe you have accomplished much more."

Jonah shrugged. "I just dug a tunnel."

"It was more than that. You trusted us, and you dug by faith. Many people would have simply walked away with the money points Matthew Coughlin gave you, but you didn't. You kept your word. That is very admirable. You are an honorable young man, and I know God has great plans for you." She looked back at the keyboard. She knew Jonah was smiling. He needed to understand his true identity. Hopefully, that would help him make the right decision when the time came.

"You are going to attack the World News?" Jonah asked.

"Yes, of sorts. I've gathered hundreds of confirmed and defaming documents against Arthur Pallue. He's been to brothels in the colonies. He's blackmailed other Efficientists. Also, Arthur Pallue's bodyguard, Bruce Rainer, has a list of illegalities behind him a mile long. It will be obvious that Arthur Pallue commanded his actions. I'm scheduling it all to start flooding the World News during the PR event."

"And that will force Arthur Pallue to command that the Kill Switch be pulled?"

"Yes," Christian nodded. "He will have no choice if he wants to keep his position of power. Done. I have it all scheduled to leak at precisely 9:15pm. We will have you waiting in the watchtower by 9:00pm or even earlier. Do you have the cartridge?"

Jonah opened the drawer of the desk. "Right here," he said, picking up the shining cartridge.

"It will take a while for the systems to reboot. As long as you get it in the Kill Switch terminal within five minutes of the lever being pulled, the virus will be planted into the systems of the World Government. There should be a light or something that glows when the upload is complete. Then…" she said, continuing to type. "Ah, here it is!"

"What?"

"This is the other virus," she said, pointing to a file on the old-style computer. "This is the second part of Matthew's plan. This part will take time."

"Like the pecan trees," Jonah said.

"Yes, years and years like the pecan trees. It can't be rushed."

"Understood," Jonah said. "I just have one question."

"Yes?"

"How will Neil Elder not see me when I put in the cartridge?"

She looked back at the computer. "Can you see the watchtower from the cabin?"

"If I go outside, I can see the light from the watchtower over the trees."

"Go outside and tell me when you see the light."

Jonah got up and walked through the backdoor entrance, leaving the door open. "I can see the light."

Christina continued typing. "How about now?"

"What? What happened?"

"What do you see now?"

"Everything went black. The light is out."

Christina quickly typed some more. "How about now?"

"The light is back on!" Jonah entered the room. "How did you do that?"

"I can control the electric grid from this computer. It truly is a secret weapon. You will hide in the vent of the watchtower with the Portable and the cartridge. Contact me right away when Neil Elder pulls the Kill Switch. I will hide in the vent at the factory and turn off the lights from there. Then I will create a diversion for him to leave the room."

"What kind of diversion?"

"I don't know yet, but it will come to me. There has to be something in the factory I can use to get him out."

"Once you upload the virus, crawl back to the vent along the factory floor and get to the computer. You see this?" she asked, pointing to the computer screen.

"Yes," he said.

"That's the electrical grid for the watchtower. Push this and the lights go off. Then push this and the lights go back on. Simple. Here try it."

Jonah did as she said.

"Good, so make sure to turn the lights back on before you crawl back through the tunnel."

"Got it," he said.

"Then make your way back to the cabin, pack everything you need into your SUV and leave. I'm not sure what's going to happen after the Kill Switch is pulled, but I believe swarms of people will be coming to the prison—researchers, more security and maybe Arthur Pallue himself. Find a place to wait out the next six months. And"— she paused—"Don't make any drastic decisions until I contact your Portable. We can set up a time and place to meet, so you can bring me the computer."

He nodded. "I promise. I won't do anything until the old-style computer is safely in your hands."

CHAPTER 11

C hristina looked at the old-style computer screen. The sound was muted, but she could see every image. She scooted down the vent, so no one would see the light of her screen through the AC duct. She doubted anyone would see it anyway. The security guards had placed a screen in the women's sleeping quarters, so they could watch the PR event. It was Christina's idea, and Neil agreed they should be able to watch such a monumental event. And the security guards were watching it upstairs in their barracks. No doubt Neil Elder was alone in the watchtower watching it from his LPS. He had no idea there was another man in the vent just above the Kill Switch watching it on his Portable.

The World News was capturing every moment of the PR event for Eve Pallue's eighteenth birthday. The young lady wore a strapless, satin gown the color of shimmering bronze that matched the color of her eyes. The skirt of the dress flowed down the back of her waist and several feet onto the floor behind her, but it came up short in the front to show her slender legs and satin bronze shoes. Her shoulder-length chestnut hair was swept back, allowing her thick gold necklace and earrings to become the focal point. She wore several chunky gold bracelets on one arm along with an elongated oval band of gold on her pointer finger. Probably millions of money points worth of gold on her—a present from her father for her birthday. She was a petite young lady, and the World News adored her. She stood next to her father and his security guard, Bruce Rainer. Her indifferent facial expression did not take away from her beauty. Finally, they left the paparazzi and went into the venue.

Christina looked at the time. The PR event was running behind. It was almost 9:05pm, and the information leak would start in ten minutes. She hoped that everyone would be sitting by then. The World News was planning on doing a visual montage of Eve's PR events through time starting with her first appearance as a baby. Little did they know that their homage to the Pallue family would turn sinister. Thankfully, she noticed that Bruce Rainer was holding a Portable. It was frowned upon to bring Portables into PR events because that time was supposed to be for growing ratings and not for building rank. She assumed the Portable was Arthur Pallue's. He would need it when the defaming information began to flow, so he could tell Neil Elder to pull the Kill Switch. He had no other choice unless he wanted over an hour's worth of information—photos, video, documents—to flow through the World News channels.

Christina set the computer down and felt for her pocket. She had retrieved cigarettes and matches from the security guard's barracks. It was difficult because the vents were smaller up there, but she crawled through the walls and took the pack of cigarettes and matches from one of the guard's nightstands. Then she crawled back up the vent. It took her several attempts, but she finally made it up. She only hoped it would be easier for Jonah. He was bigger than she, but he was also much stronger. She had figured out how to create a diversion once the Kill Switch was pulled. She had a pile of dry cotton ready right under Neil Elder's window. She poured oil onto it, and she only hoped it was enough. With the lights out, he would see her fire burning bright.

She looked back at the screen. The visual show had started. "One minute left," she whispered. Her heart began to pound. So many things could go wrong, but this was the last risk she and Jonah would have to take for a long time. She thought of Jonah and silently prayed that he did not bring his gun with him. It would be easy for him to shoot Neil Elder with the lights out, but Jonah had made a promise. He always kept his promises. She noticed movement from the crowd of Efficientists sitting at their adorned round tables. The information leak had begun. Arthur Pallue stood up and was yelling at the master of ceremonies, but he looked just as confused as everyone else. Images of Arthur Pallue with naked women moved across the screen. Documents to magistrates from the other regions of the World Government appeared with names and amounts highlighted. A video of Bruce Rainer pushing down an Efficientist long retired with Arthur Pallue standing by looped two times. Though she couldn't hear it, she knew Bruce was threating the man. She had heard the video numerous times since it was she who created this little montage to Arthur Pallue's corruption.

"Come on," Christina willed. "Get your Portable and make the call."

Arthur Pallue turned to Bruce and got his Portable. Then he pointed at his daughter, and Bruce grabbed her arm and pulled her out of her seat. He led her out of the venue.

"I guess the birthday girl is going home," she whispered.

The audience didn't notice as Arthur Pallue got on his Portable because they were too enthralled in the video. However, one of the paparazzi from the World News kept a camera on him, capturing his reaction. His face beamed red.

"Make the call," Christina said under her breath. She knew he didn't want all this information to get out. He needed to stop it. She stared at the spot of the screen for communication. She needed Jonah to contact her.

Finally, Jonah's update appeared on her screen in capital letters: *KILL SWITCH PULLED.* Christina quickly typed on the keyboard. "Lights out," she whispered, setting the computer down and crawling back to the entrance of the vent to listen. It was quiet. She opened it and slid out, moving the vent back over the hole. She ran to the entrance of the factory. She had made sure it was unlocked before she crawled into the vent. She pushed the door open and sprinted straight to the pile of cotton. She lit a match, but the wind blew it out. She crouched closer to the pile of cotton and lit another match. The flame stayed, so she dropped it on the fluffy pile of white. The cotton went up in flames. "Whoa, maybe I put too much oil on it."

Then she took out the pack of cigarettes and lit one. She had never smoked before, but she needed to look like she knew what she was doing. She inhaled deeply and coughed. She inhaled again. Then she began to walk back to the factory door. Neil was waiting for her with his Portable under his arm.

"What the hell are you doing?"

"I'm smoking. What does it look like I'm doing?"

"You put our damn cotton on fire!"

"I know. I didn't mean too. I guess I was smoking too close to the pile, and the ash of the cigarette must have fallen on it."

Neil Elder put his hands on his face. "Christina Straight you are infuriating!"

Officer Evans came through the factory door and stopped abruptly when he noticed the fire. "Sir, the cotton is on fire!"

"Don't you think I know that you idiot! Go get the others and put it out!"

"Yes, sir," he said and ran back into the factory.

"What are you doing out here?" Neil demanded.

Christina spread out her arms. "You said I was free to walk the grounds of the prison."

"Where did you get those cigarettes from?"

She looked at the cigarette in her hand. "I stole them from one of the officers, but I fully intend to repay him with money points when I get out."

He placed his hands on his hips. "You smoke? I don't believe it."

She threw the cigarette on the ground and put the light out with her shoe. "Only occasionally, but I was craving one. They were just there in the kitchen. I didn't think it was a big deal."

Neil looked up to the watchtower when the lights blinked back on. "The lights on are the fritz. Someone attacked the World News. The cotton is on fire. This factory has become a nightmare!"

"What happened to the World News?"

He looked at her. "You weren't watching?"

"No, I told you. I was out here smoking. I don't want to watch a PR event for Arthur Pallue's daughter."

"The World News was attacked with false information about Arthur Pallue. Simple as that." He looked down at his Portable. The screen glowed, and he gave several commands. He exhaled and smiled. "But all seems to be well. We stopped the attack, and the World Government systems are intact."

"Why are you smiling?" She knew the answer to her question. He had pulled the Kill Switch and his design worked. They now knew that they had a failsafe to protect the World Government.

His smile instantly faded. Then the security guards rushed past them. The lead security guard was holding a fire extinguisher while the others held buckets of water. Simultaneously, they sprayed white dust and water all over the burning cotton and the fire hissed to a halt.

Neil looked back at his Portable. "Officer Evans, come here!"

The lead guard handed the fire extinguisher to another guard and walked back to where they were standing.

"Yes, sir," he said.

"I want all the privileges of the prisoners taken away, especially for this one. From now on, they will be treated like Colonial prisoners. They will work. They will eat. And they will sleep. They must be monitored every moment, including night security. I just got word that Arthur Pallue himself will be here in a few days with a team of researchers, and we will not let them see this circus we have created here!"

"Yes, sir," Officer Evans said.

Neil turned to Christina Straight. "And you will serve your six months by staying out of my way. I'll make sure that your rank is greatly reduced for the mockery you have made of me."

"I understand," she said, handing him the matches and cigarettes. "I want to return these."

He grabbed them out of her hand and threw them on the ground. "Now get back to your quarters. You have a hard day of work shoveling burnt cotton tomorrow. In fact, you have six months of hard labor to look forward to!"

Christina walked back toward the factory door with Neil Elder following behind her. She couldn't help the grin that spread across her face. It worked. The first part of Matthew Coughlin's plan was complete. Now time was on her side to implement the second part. And most importantly, Jonah was safe. He had turned the lights of the watchtower back on, so that meant he was back at his cabin getting ready to leave. He had already packed his SUV. She envisioned him carrying his Portable and the old-style computer and stowing them safely in the SUV. He needed to leave soon, especially since Arthur Pallue and his team would be coming. She would see him again—even if for only a minute to get the computer back. As she entered the factory, she silently prayed that Jonah would give up his plan of revenge and embrace God's new plan of hope.

Jonah placed the old-style computer onto the small refrigerator that rested against the back wall of his cabin. Then he carefully placed his Portable on it. He felt the gun against his thigh in his pant pocket. With shaking hands, he fished out his keys from the other pocket. He had brought the gun with him. He told himself it was for protection, but inside he knew it was a lie. As he unlocked the backdoor of the cabin, he went over what happened in his mind.

Neil Elder was alone in the watchtower watching the PR event for Eve Pallue. The other guards were in their barracks watching. Quickly, though, the call from Arthur Pallue came. The call to pull the Kill Switch. Jonah waited. He didn't breathe as Neil Elder opened the case surrounding the Kill Switch and turned the key to unlock it. Neil paused momentarily but then quickly grabbed the red lever with both hands and pulled. He walked over to his desk and turned on his LPS. The screen was black. Jonah sent the okay to turn off the lights. That's when everything went dark. Neil Elder cursed and began looking for his Portable. Jonah set his Portable aside and picked up his gun with his right hand and the cartridge in the other. He wanted Neil to see him, so he would have a reason to break his promise to Miss Christina.

Then a bright light was seen from a distance, and Neil walked to the window. That was the diversion that Miss Christina had planned.

Jonah moved the vent to the AC duct out away from the entrance. He leaned his head and arm out and pointed his gun at Neil Elder's head. In his mind, he thought he could easily shoot him, but he had never actually shot the gun. He only did dry fire practices. He just needed Neil to turn around and see him. But he saw Miss Christina's figure through the window. She was outside next to a pile of cotton on fire. If he shot Neil Elder, she would be blamed as an accomplice. By getting his revenge, he would be hurting her. He brought his arm and head back into the AC duct. He wasn't a killer. He was a protector, and right now, Christina Straight needed him.

Neil Elder left the window holding his Portable. He cursed some more and made his way to the door of the watchtower and left. That's when Jonah went into action. He shimmied out of the AC duct and landed on the top of a desk. Then he hurried to the kill switch and found the terminal. He pushed in the cartridge and waited. He had no clue how long the upload would take. Moments later, the light on the terminal beamed green. Then he took out the cartridge and hurried to the AC duct. It was much more difficult to get back up into the vent. He heard voices outside. Security guards were putting the flames out. He needed to hurry. Finally, he made his way up. He crawled through the vent of the AC making his way down to the bottom floor. That's where he found the old-style computer waiting for him. He clicked the button that Miss Christina showed him, hoping the lights to the watchtower would come back on. Then he grabbed the computer and Portable and traveled through the dark tunnel one last time.

When Jonah made it into the cabin, it was almost empty. He had already packed everything in his SUV, which was waiting for him in the makeshift garage he built around it. He had just forgotten one thing. He went into his room, and there by his nightstand was his pappa's old tacklebox with his mother's family's photos. He grabbed it. Then he looked around one last time. This was no longer his home. He would find a new home that suited him better. He had six months to prepare a new life for himself. Then he went back outside and carefully put the computer, Portable and gun into the tacklebox. He left the keys to the cabin on the refrigerator. Maybe another family in the Colonies would find this place and make a home of it. He was headed to the city. That's where his future life would begin.

CHAPTER 12

Jonah stood next to his family's gravesite. He hadn't stared upon the gravestones in months since the night the Kill Switch was pulled. He placed the tacklebox in his *freedom grave* as Uncle Matt had called it. The tunnel hidden in that grave truly had become a path to his freedom, digging it and carrying out his part of the plan through it. The tacklebox and his family's photos would be safe there. He couldn't take the past with him into his new life, but he would keep the Goodman name. That was the one part of his family's legacy he wouldn't let go of.

He thought of his walk here. He couldn't believe his make-shift garage was still there. He parked his SUV and made his way through the forest one last time. On his way here, he snuck by his old cabin, and he was right. A couple with a young baby and toddler lived there now. He made sure that they didn't see him. He had long since discovered that he intimidated people with his size. The pecan tree was growing strong, as well. Hopefully, it would supply the young family with a small harvest soon It made his heart happy thinking about the little kids picking up the pecans and cracking them for a midday snack.

He turned back to his father's gravestone. "I'm sorry I haven't visited in a long while. You all missed my birthday, but I bought myself something really nice. Papa, you would be proud of me, and you too, Mamma. Well, this is goodbye. I don't think I'll be able to visit you very often. My new job will keep me away, but I know you would be proud of me. I've learned so much and grown in my head and heart—and body," he laughed. He leaned down and placed a bullet on his father's grave. "This is the revenge I wanted for you, but I'm giving it to you now. I believe your life and the lives of Mamma, Isaiah and Maureen will be vindicated, not because I used that bullet, but because I didn't. And don't worry," he said patting the gun at his hip. "I have plenty more bullets now, and I know how to shoot them correctly."

He looked toward the graves of his mamma and siblings. He had gathered wildflowers and placed them upon their gravestones. "I will miss you all, but I will always carry you in my heart. When the final part of Uncle Matt's plan is accomplished, your deaths will share in a grand design to free all people from the tyranny we experienced. I promise you. I will do everything in my power to be there when it happens."

He looked at the gold watch wrapped around his thick, dark wrist. "I better be going. I have a date with a friend. I love you all, and I will see you one day when you greet me at the heavenly gates." With that, Jonah turned and made his way back to his SUV hidden in the forest.

Christina Straight stood near her designated security van surrounded by more than sixty women ready to get back to civilization. There were ten vans in all and over twenty security guards. Neil Elder left the factory with his team over a month ago. The new factory director, Raul Jimenez, was a middle-aged and ambitious Efficientists. He brought his own team of security with him and worked with Neil Elder for a few weeks before taking over the position full time. Now that Arthur Pallue knew the Kill Switch worked, the factory would become an invaluable commodity to him. However, all news about the Kill Switch was kept secret.

She doubted Arthur Pallue had yet to tell the other regions of the World Government about it. She would do some research when she returned home. She looked to her left at her new friend, Lisa. "I'm ready to get back to my condo in the city. I want to sleep in my own bed, water my plants and resume helping my clients."

"Me too," Lisa said. "I can't believe they are sending us all home after six months. I know you only had six months to serve, but I had a year to serve. Some of the women had even more time."

"I guess they want to get us all out and erase the fact that they ever established a women's prison for Efficientists so far away from the city," Christina mused, thinking about Matthew Coughlin who arranged the entire thing through the old-style computer.

"Their loss is our gain," Lisa said.

Lisa had been a home nurse in the city until she got caught skimming pills from her patients. She had numerous personal issues she needed to deal with, and Christina was more than happy to use her Life Therapy skills while she served her sentence at the prison. In fact, she had learned a lot and was able to implement much of her knowledge in various ways.

Lisa continued. "When I get back, I will get my probation time over with and get my full nursing license redeemed. No more pills for me." Lisa leaned into Christina and gave her a big hug. "I know I've said this a million times, but you really helped me work through my problems. I was using drugs to cover up so much pain. I am glad I was discovered stealing and sentenced at this prison where I found you. Otherwise, I think things would have gotten much worse back in the city."

Christina squeezed her back. "And you can call my LPS anytime. Remember that."

"I will, and not always for therapy. I want to keep up with my friend."

Christina heard movement on the road beyond the fence. A large black SUV drove up to the gate and stopped. One of the security guards with a Portable walked to the gate. He checked his Portable for over a minute. The driver of the vehicle got out of the SUV carrying his Portable. Christina recognized the driver instantly. It was Jonah. "Oh no," she whispered.

Lisa turned. "What's wrong?"

Christina quickly recovered. "Oh, it's just that I want to go home, and I hope that situation won't delay us."

Lisa looked to where the security guard was talking to the driver. "I'm sure it has nothing to do with us. At least, I hope it doesn't."

The driver went back to his SUV, and the security guard opened the gate. "He's coming in," Christina whispered shaking her head. She hoped Jonah knew that Neil Elder was gone. There would be no revenge for him today. He should have waited like she said until she contacted him. The SUV slowly drove up and parked next to one of the security vans. The security guard who opened the gate walked toward her until they were face-to-face.

"Are you Christina Straight?" he asked.

"Yes, sir."

"Your bodyguard is here to retrieve you. He has clearance to take you home."

She knew her countenance appeared shocked. "Sorry, yes. I had hoped he would get approval, but I wasn't sure."

"Wow. I didn't realize you were such a high ranking Efficientist," Lisa said under her breath.

"What's going on here?" a voice boomed. It was Raul Jimenez, the new factory director. He walked sharply toward her.

"Sorry, sir. I just got orders that Christina Straight would be escorted home by her bodyguard," the security guard said, holding out his Portable.

"Let me see that." Director Jimenez placed his Portable under his arm and took the security guard's. He read the screen for several seconds. "Here," he said, shoving the Portable back into the man's hands. Then he held out his Portable and gave short commands while reading the screen. "How is that possible? Send the bodyguard to me."

"Yes, sir." The security guard walked to the SUV.

Christina's stomach tightened as she watched. They had almost gotten away with it all, and now Jonah was jeopardizing the entire plan. She silently prayed he didn't have the old-style computer in the SUV in case it got confiscated. Jonah got out of the car with his Portable. He wore a dark blue pinstriped suit with a yellow shirt and blue tie. He had on brown leather shoes and belt and wore aviator sunglasses. Christina couldn't believe it. Jonah really did look like a bodyguard. He walked straight to the director and stretched out his hand.

"Director Jimenez, my name is Jonah Goodman the Third," he said with his bass voice. He firmly shook the director's hand, revealing the open-carry pistol on his hip. "I am Christina Straight's bodyguard. Sorry I have been delayed. Neil Elder asked to dispatch me yesterday, but the paperwork never got sent from his office. He needs Christina Straight back in the city ASAP."

"Neil Elder sent you to pick up a prisoner?" the director asked, skeptically.

"You have the paperwork on your Portable, do you not? Would you like me to interrupt Neil Elder's research and let him talk with you?"

Director Jimenez looked back down at his Portable. "No," he said, clearing this throat. "Don't bother him. This is just unexpected. What is your name again?"

"Jonah. Goodman. The Third," he enunciated.

The director looked at his Portable again. "Christina Straight is your first assignment?"

"Yes," Jonah answered.

"It's unusual for a prisoner to leave without being processed back at the security station in the city."

Jonah pulled down his sunglasses to get a good look at the director. "If you would look at your paperwork more closely, you would find that Christina Straight has already been processed. She is free to go. In fact, I can report you for detaining an Efficientist who is needed back in the city. You are openly violating her right to produce at this very moment going against Arthur Pallue's *Life Efficiency*."

Christina could tell that the director's breathing quickened. He looked down at his Portable once more and swiped the screen a few times. "I see it now. My apologies. Please, don't bother Neil Elder with this minor mishap. You both are free to leave."

Jonah pushed his sunglasses back in place. "Thank you. I'll let Neil Elder know that you were more than accommodating." Then for the first time, he looked at her. "Miss Christina, it is time to go home." He grabbed her bag and held out his arm. She placed her palm behind his elbow and let him lead her to the SUV. He opened the back passenger door and helped her onto her seat and handed her the bag. Then he went around the front, nodded to the director and got into the driver's seat.

"Buckle up, Miss Christina. We have a long drive ahead of us."

Christina said nothing until they were through the gate. "Jonah, how did you do all that?"

He smiled as he drove. "You didn't know you hired me?"

She laughed. "Of course not!"

"I've had time to practice on the old-style computer. It comes in handy when you need to make things happen."

"I can tell you've been doing a lot of studying. You sound like an Efficientist."

"A low-ranking one," he said. "But that is fine with me."

"How could you possibly enlist Neil Elder's help? Did you fake those documents?"

"Not at all," Jonah said, as he turned onto the main road. "As your bodyguard, I reminded Neil Elder that you were needed back home to intercept the information you had ready to send to Arthur Pallue."

"Oh," she said. "Well, there was never any documentation of our therapy sessions. I lied to him to ensure that I would make it home safely."

"I figured as much, but who was I to question my employer?"

"Jonah, you truly want to work with me?" she asked. She had hoped, but the crossover from Colonial life to a life as an Efficientist was difficult for some people.

"I'm almost out of money points, so I do need employment," he said.

"What happened to your money?" He couldn't have possibly spent all of it in the Colonies without becoming suspicious to others.

"I hope you don't think I was presumptuous, but I bought a condo in your building. If I'm going to protect you, I need to be close. I didn't realize how expensive those homes were. It took almost every money point Uncle Matt gave me, but I think he would like it."

Christina leaned back in her seat. She realized Jonah had made a major life decision, and she was proud of him. "So, you turned eighteen, you are officially a licensed bodyguard, you have a condo in the city, and now you have employment."

"Yes, ma'am. And I've been practicing with my gun at the shooting range. I'm a good shot. I think I will make an excellent bodyguard."

"Plus, you are trustworthy, and you keep your promises. I would love for you to be my bodyguard, Jonah

Goodman the Third." Then she stopped. "Didn't Neil Elder recognize your name?"

Jonah shook his head. "Neil Elder only knew us as numbers. He rarely looked at us. We weren't his priority. I talked to him directly on his LPS, and he had absolutely no recollection of me, which I knew he wouldn't."

"You made your peace with him?" Christina asked.

Jonah gave a mischievous grin. "I wouldn't say that, but I know that all vengeance is the Lord's. I trust that Neil Elder will pay for his crimes. Until then, we have a second part of my Uncle Matt's plan to finish."

"That will take time," Christina reminded him.

"Yep, and during this time I will live each day as a free man."

"Indeed," she said.

CHAPTER 13

Christina eyed the last of her vegetable alfredo but was too full to take another bite. She and Jonah sat at a table in the patio of a small bistro café near their condo complex. Many lower ranked Efficientists frequented the restaurant. She enjoyed eating there because the paparazzi didn't loiter at that location, and she rarely bumped into any of her clients, most of whom were higher ranked Efficientists. Jonah had to interact with the Efficientists and their bodyguards when they came to her condo office for face-to-face therapy sessions to avoid being tracked on the world-web. He had shown himself to be exceedingly proficient and likeable—if not rather intimidating.

"How's the studying going for the next stage of your bodyguard licensing?" she asked.

Jonah stretched against the back of his chair and placed his fork on the plate where a large New York strip and loaded baked potato once rested before he devoured them. "I had to catch up on the first part of the license that Uncle Matt gifted me, but I'm learning quickly. I took the intro exam and passed. It felt good to know that I have now earned the title as your bodyguard—instead of cheating my way into it."

"Don't forget," Christina said, "God often cheats for His children."

He sighed. "I know. Like you always say, I am highly favored, but I also want to serve a purpose. I firmly believe that being the best bodyguard I can be is part of that purpose."

Christina smiled and nodded. He had integrity and a good heart. She was glad they found each other; though, her first choice would have not been meeting at a prison in the Colonies.

The pair spoke no words for several minutes. The wind of the city had turned unseasonably cold, but the coolness was a pleasant surprise.

"Do you miss it?" Jonah asked.

Christina looked at the young man who had now become her closest confidant. He had matured beyond his years. Trauma could either destroy a life or recreate a stronger one, and he had transformed before her eyes for the better. She glanced side to side to make sure no one was in ear shot and leaned forward. "Do I miss getting on the old-style computer and snooping?"

He nodded.

"Yes, but it is only right. It is too tempting to eavesdrop and go places and change things I shouldn't. No one should have that much power. If I keep using it, they'll eventually figure it out. The first part of the plan is in place, and I think the second will take a lot more people, but I trust God will bring everyone together like He did us."

"But you're having to publish your faith writings the old way," Jonah said. "It's more dangerous, and the bread trail may eventually lead to you."

"It's a risk I am always willing to take. God has always protected me except for when He wanted me to be found out," she said, thinking about her time in prison. "Plus, I have a feeling the computer will go into another person's hands. It doesn't feel like mine, and I guess it never did. God has a purpose for it, so it needs to stay hidden until then."

"Do you think Eve Pallue still may play a role in future events?" Jonah asked.

Christina thought of the expressionless young lady she had seen at the PR event wearing her glittery bronze gown. "Most definitely, but I don't know what side she'll play on. I know she's working on a new Life Plan."

"Let's just hope she's part of the good ending," Jonah said.

"I think she could, but something has to happen to wake her up from her sleep."

"And when it does, we will be here," Jonah added.

"Yes, we will. As long as it takes, we will be here ready for her."

Onoma Series:
Eve of Awakening: Book 1
Bear into Redemption: Book 2
Mark within Salvation: Book 3
Hunt for Understanding: Book 4
Straight to Eternity: Prequel Novella

I hope you enjoyed this fiction series. If you like this book, please write a quick review on Amazon. Also, if you enjoy my writing, check out my other non-fiction and fiction works on my website, www.alisahopewagner.com.

www.ingramcontent.com/pod-product-compliance
Lightning Source LLC
Chambersburg PA
CBHW070605180626
46817CB00005B/1999